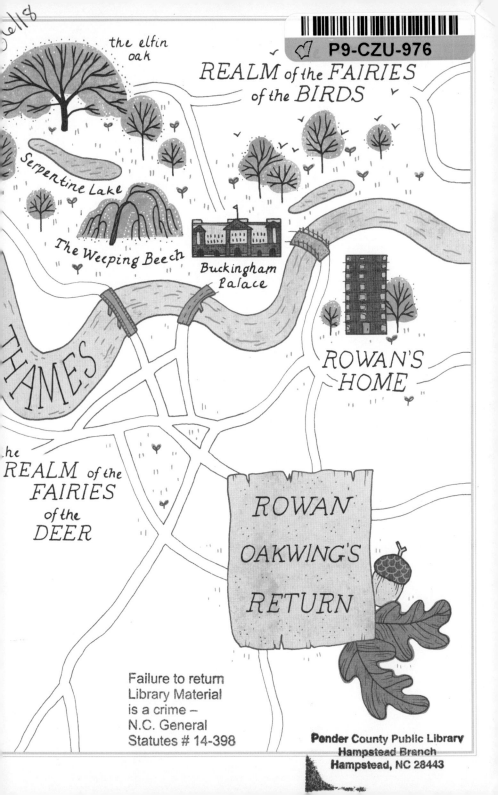

OAKWING

A Fairy's Courage

DON'T MISS WHERE
THE ADVENTURE BEGAN!

Oakwing: A Fairy's Tale

OAKWING

A Fairy's Courage

- Book 2 -

E.J. Clarke

Aladdin
New York   London   Toronto   Sydney   New Delhi

ALADDIN

An imprint of Simon & Schuster Children's Publishing Division
1230 Avenue of the Americas, New York, New York 10020
First Aladdin hardcover edition May 2018
Text copyright © 2018 by E. J. Clarke
Jacket illustrations copyright © 2018 by Jori van der Linde

For information about special discounts for bulk purchases, please contact
Simon & Schuster Special Sales at 1-866-506-1949 or business@simonandschuster.com.
The Simon & Schuster Speakers Bureau can bring authors to your live event. For more information or to book an event, contact the Simon & Schuster Speakers Bureau at 1-866-248-3049 or visit our website at www.simonspeakers.com.
Jacket designed by Jessica Handelman
Interior designed by Mike Rosamilia
The text of this book was set in Scala OT.
Manufactured in the United States of America 0418 FFG
2 4 6 8 10 9 7 5 3 1
Library of Congress Cataloging-in-Publication Data
Names: Clarke, E. J., author.
Title: A fairy's courage / by E. J. Clarke.
Description: First Aladdin hardcover edition. | New York : Aladdin, 2018. |
Series: Oakwing ; book two | Summary: When her mother is kidnapped by evil fairy
Vulpes and his army of foxes, Rowan, her fairy friends, and a tiger from the
London Zoo set out to save her and the fairy realms.
Identifiers: LCCN 2017034064 (print) | LCCN 2017049622 (eBook) |
ISBN 9781481481953 (eBook) | ISBN 9781481481946 (hc)
Subjects: | CYAC: Fairy tales. | Fairies—Fiction. | Adventure and adventurers—Fiction. |
Family life—Fiction. | Kidnapping—Fiction. | Foxes—Fiction. | Tigers—Fiction. |
London (England)—Fiction. | England—Fiction.
Classification: LCC PZ8.C547 (eBook) | LCC PZ8.C547 Fai 2018 (print) |
DDC [Fic]—3dc23
LC record available at https://lccn.loc.gov/2017034064

For Rose
and Miriam

OAKWING
A Fairy's Courage

* Chapter One *
THE FAMILY OUTING

"She's alive, Dad! And she loves you. She wanted me to tell you."

Rowan was so full of hope and excitement, it positively burst out of her.

"But . . ."

It was too much for her father to take in all at once.

"*Dad.* We have to find a way to bring her back. . . ."

Rowan looked up at her father to see his eyes opened wide in shock.

The morning sunshine was flooding through the windows high up in their block of apartments. Rowan could see her mom's chair in its familiar position—not facing the television like all the others but facing out the window, out across the rooftops of the city and far into the distance. Toward Hyde Park and Kensington Gardens. The parks that had been her mother's escape from the worries of her life before she'd disappeared from theirs, all those seven long years ago. Rowan sat herself down in her mother's chair, and her dad and sister gathered around her.

"Slowly, Rowan," said her father. "Tell us what happened to you."

"It's the parks, Dad," said Rowan. "All the Royal Parks of London. They're not really parks at all. They're . . . sanctuaries."

"What do you mean?" said Dad, looking puzzled.

There was no easy way to say it, so she just came right out with it.

"Sanctuaries . . . for fairies."

Willow's face immediately lit up in excitement. "Fairies!"

But Rowan was trying to read the look on her dad's face. It had immediately tensed.

"Rowan, it's been a long few days for you. We've been going mad with worry here."

"Yes, yes, it has, but please let me explain. I know it sounds crazy—"

"It sounds fabulous!" said Willow, not entirely helpfully.

"Promise me you'll hear me out, Dad. Just let me tell you the truth."

Dad took Rowan's hand and slowly nodded. Willow sat on the floor cross-legged like she was back in the story corner at school, beaming with anticipation. Rowan took a deep breath, and the whole story spilled out of her like toys falling from an overstuffed cupboard—not necessarily in the right order.

"It was Queen Victoria who started it, back in the olden days. She knew about the fairies and so she created the parks to protect them from all the people and the pollution of the city. It was Harold who told me that. He's a . . . robin."

"A talking robin?" gasped Willow.

"Harold told me how I had become a fairy—"

"You . . . WERE A FAIRY?" said Willow, practically shouting with excitement.

Rowan knew how this was sounding. She realized it seemed like a fantastical story to Willow, and complete nonsense to her dad. But she'd lived it and knew that it had really happened. So she pressed on.

"Yes. I cried beneath the weeping beech in Hyde Park and fell asleep. When I woke up, I was a fairy. Harold said that"—Rowan knew this next bit might be hard for Dad to hear—"it was because I felt nobody cared about me after Mom disappeared. That's how people become fairies. That's how Mom did."

Rowan waited anxiously for her father's response. She hadn't wanted to hurt his feelings, but it was the truth. Finally he spoke.

"You went all the way to Hyde Park by yourself? Is that where you've been all this time?"

Rowan's shoulders dropped. He obviously hadn't believed a word. Willow, on the other hand, had read enough books to know that life was generally a lot more exciting than grown-ups made out.

"What about Mom? She was a fairy too?"

Rowan turned back to the only person who seemed to want to hear this story.

"Yes. Yes, she was a fairy too. And she still is. She's trapped in Bushy Park on the other side of London. That's why we have to find a way to get her back."

Willow was already on her feet.

"Let's go now!"

"Hold your horses, madam," said Dad, throwing out an arm to sit Willow back down with a *thump*. "Rowan, you've been missing for days. I had to call the police, so first I have to tell them that you're okay. I know you miss your mom. We all do. But this? I need to know what *really* happened to you. Just to put my mind at rest. Please."

Rowan slumped back into her chair. There was no time to waste if she was going to get Mom back, and she really needed all the help she could get. She knew there was a chance that the thing she wanted most in the world could really happen, that their family could be whole again. But how was she ever going to explain? And what she'd told them so far wasn't even the half of it. In fairness, she wouldn't have believed it herself if she'd been the one doing the listening. She gazed back out the window at the parks in the distance, and something clicked in her brain. She held her wooden pendant out to show him, her acorn now fixed within the oak tree charm that had belonged to her mother.

"Where did you get that?" Dad asked, taken aback.

"Let me show you," said Rowan. "I'll retrace my

steps, and you can see for yourself what happened. From the beginning."

Dad narrowed his eyes, and Rowan could see his mind whirring. Her father's work had something to do with computers, and he liked everything to be explained "by rational means." So after all the talk of fairies, this must have seemed like a pretty reasonable suggestion.

"FAMILY OUTING!" shouted Willow.

Dad gave in. "Okay," he said. "Tomorrow. First you need a hot bath, a proper meal, and a good night's sleep, young lady. And I have to let everyone know you're safe. There's a lot of people who have been very worried about you. The outing can wait till then."

"*Please* can we go this afternoon?" pleaded Rowan. "There's no telling what might happen to Mom. There's foxes, there's Jack Pike, there's Vulpes . . ."

Rowan trailed off. Maybe that was too much information for one day.

"Who's Jack?" asked Willow brightly. "What's a Vulpes?"

Rowan winced. Fortunately, Dad wasn't listening again. At least not to the bits that mattered.

"Absolutely not, Rowan. We're not going anywhere today. We're spending the day safe and sound in the apartment. Tomorrow you can show us everything."

Rowan accepted that was the best she could expect for now. She would have to convince her dad in the place where it all happened tomorrow. Back in the parks. The place she knew now as the Fairy Realms.

The next day Rowan was back on the top deck of the bus, sweeping through the London streets as the long summer shadows stretched around her. She remembered very well how she'd felt the last time she'd taken this journey. Full of sadness and feeling more alone than ever. But this time she wasn't by herself. She had an excited little sister and a skeptical father for company. As their dad sat behind them looking out the window, Willow leaned in to whisper into her sister's ear.

"What was she like?"

Willow had been only two years old when their mother had disappeared from their lives, and Willow was frequently upset by the fact that she couldn't remember anything about her mom. Rowan took her gently by the hand.

"She was playing a violin made from reeds, and she was wearing a crown made from willow twigs, and she was so beautiful and kind and . . ."

Rowan trailed off when she saw that Willow's eyes were scrunched up tight, desperately trying to picture the scene in her mind.

"Don't stop!" said Willow.

Rowan knew how much this meant to her. And that knowledge weighed heavily on her mind.

"You're going to see her for yourself, Willow."

"Promise?"

Rowan felt the weight get heavier still. But she nodded all the same.

They jumped off the bus at Hyde Park Corner, and Rowan raced through the park. Willow skipped at her heels, and Dad had to do a kind of running walk just to keep up with his two girls. They arrived at the Elfin Oak and peered through the railings that protected it. Just as before, there were all manner of colorful painted fairy-tale creatures carved into its trunk.

"So, this is what I did first," said Rowan. "I looked at the little blue fairy there with two shells for wings— just like I did the last time we came here with Mom."

"I remember!" cried Willow.

"You were too young to remember, Willow," said Dad.

"And then I looked over at the clock tower where we used to sit with Mom, and there was another mother there. And that made the sadness come back."

Dad crouched down. "It's okay, Rowan. I think I'm starting to get the picture."

"You are?"

Dad started to circle the oak and began to speak a bit like one of those detectives on television when they were solving a mystery.

"You were missing Mom, Rowan, and you were feeling lonely, so you came to the park. To be in the last place where you'd been with her before she disappeared."

Rowan nodded. He seemed to be getting it.

"You walked around the Elfin Oak, like this, and you looked at all of these little fairy-tale creatures. Just like that blue fairy there. A little *fairy* Rowan. And look, there's an elf, and a wise old bird . . . and it took you back, straight back to the moment when you were last here with Mom. But then you saw the other mother sitting in your place, and you were already feeling terribly sad, and that just made things ten times worse."

Rowan nodded a little more slowly this time. She wasn't sure where he was going with this anymore.

"So you got yourself away from here. And your heart was hurting, and your head was full of fairies and elves and Mom, and it all got mixed up and churned around inside you like in a washing machine. And you fell asleep under that tree like you said. . . ."

Dad came back and held Rowan's hands, his eyes meeting hers.

"And you had this most wonderful *dream*."

Rowan felt tears coming to her eyes, but she refused to let them out and blinked them back down. She scrunched up her face and shook her head, too emotional to speak for a moment. When she did talk, her voice croaked a bit.

"What about this, Dad?" She held up the necklace that had been tucked beneath her dress. "It belonged to Mom, didn't it? And now I have it, because everything I've told you is *true*. The fairies called this pendant 'the Heart of Oak.' They thought it was part of a prophecy, that '*When the fairy of most power unlocks the Heart of Oak, they shall become human again.*' And here I am!"

Rowan's dad did one of those sad-happy smiles

that parents do when they don't believe you but don't want to hurt your feelings.

"You've always been a human, Rowan, and it's just a necklace. You could have gotten it . . . anywhere."

Rowan squeezed the oak pendant in her hands, as if to prove she still believed it was more than that. But the lump in her throat was proof that her father didn't.

"Come to the tree, Dad?" Rowan asked quietly. "To the weeping beech? Before we go home? That's where I went next."

"Of course, Rowan. Let's go and see the tree. We still have a little time."

Dad clearly thought she was making everything up. He thought it was a silly little story she was telling to make herself feel better. She knew how it sounded, but still she had to convince him. How else would they be able to get Mom back?

With Dad hanging behind them savoring his early evening summer stroll, Rowan walked hand in hand with Willow across the park, along the length of the Serpentine Lake.

"The bobbily boats!" shouted Willow.

Rowan smiled. "You *do* remember, Willow Pillow!"

"That's what I said, didn't I?"

"Do you believe me, Willow?"

"Of course!"

Rowan squeezed Willow's hand a little tighter.

"You're a terrible liar, for a start. You're such a Goody Two-shoes," said Willow, squeezing Rowan's hand back. "I'd know in a second if you were making it up."

They rounded the lake, toward the café where they'd bought ice creams the last time they'd been here with their mother.

"Pink ice cream!" cried Willow.

Rowan dragged her reluctantly past the window as Willow gazed longingly into it, and then they turned the corner to find the little dell where the majestic weeping beech stood behind its railing.

At least it looked like the weeping beech that Rowan's tears had seeped into, the tree that had transformed her into a fairy. But even though it was the middle of summer, the beech had no leaves at all. Something, or someone, had stripped it completely bare.

* Chapter Two *

IT IS WHAT IT IS

"What in the Realms?" cried Rowan in horror. Dad caught up with her and Willow. "It was that tree. The one with no leaves. I sat under there and fell asleep. And when I woke up, I was a fairy."

"I think someone would have seen you, Rowan," replied her dad softly.

"But it was *covered* in leaves then. It was like a huge green tent to hide in. No one saw me!"

Rowan's dad did that happy-sad smile again.

"Someone's done something awful to the poor tree, Dad. It must be Vulpes."

"Vulpes? Is that some kind of disease? Something *has* happened to it, Rowan. But *someone*? I think it's time we went home, love."

"Vulpes rules over the fairies and the foxes of

Greenwich Park. And he doesn't like me one bit."

Rowan's dad looked mystified, but Rowan had stopped caring how this all sounded. There was work to be done. She pushed forward to the railing, and with a quick glance left and right, she started to climb over.

"Rowan, what are you doing?" said her dad, catching her arm and pulling her back down. "Look, why don't we go and grab one of those pink ice creams you used to like so much before we go?"

"Ice cream time!" cried Willow.

"Thanks, Dad, but I—I just want to sit here for a bit." Rowan plonked herself on a nearby bench. Dad took Willow's hand and set off for the café.

"We'll be back in a little while," he said, looking over his shoulder at Rowan. "But stay here, okay?"

Now it was Rowan's turn to do one of the happy-sad smiles as she watched them disappear. As soon as they were inside the café, she jumped up again and went straight back to the railing. She hopped over without a second thought and sneaked up to the tree. Standing at the base of the giant beech, she gazed up and down it, searching for clues that might suggest what had done this. But there was nothing to tell her. Only a single, last forlorn leaf spiraling down from above to land on her shoulder. *The tree's crying,* thought Rowan, remembering what Willow used to say about the weeping beech. Rowan reached out to hug it, in case that might make it feel better. As she closed her eyes and squeezed the tree tightly, she felt something land on her other shoulder, and she reflexively swished her hand to brush it away. But the thing wasn't another leaf, and it didn't take kindly to being swatted.

"Charming!" cried the thing that wasn't a leaf but was in fact Harold the robin.

"Harold!"

The bird hovered warily in the air next to her.

"You're not going to hit me again, are you? I have to say I preferred you when you were much smaller. . . ."

"Come here, you silly bird," said Rowan, reaching out to cup him in her hands.

"Ouch," said Harold as Rowan slightly squashed him in her eagerness.

"Does that old broken wing still hurt you?" said Rowan, holding him back out to look at him. And then she noticed how bedraggled Harold was looking.

Bits of downy feather were hanging off him, and he seemed tired and worn-out.

"What happened, Harold? To you? To the beech?"

Harold took a deep breath, but the voices of people passing nearby stopped him from speaking. He and Rowan had to be sure that no one was going to see a robin talking to a girl. With a last glance in the direction of the café, Rowan and Harold crept around to the back of the tree's great trunk and down into the little dell beyond, then hid themselves in a bush by a babbling stream.

"It's Vulpes," said Harold, confirming Rowan's suspicions. "Once he'd found the way into Jack's underground palace the first time, it didn't take long for him to return. He came at night, while everyone was asleep."

Harold took a breath, as if he were about to deliver some bad news. Rowan leaned forward, expecting the worst.

"Is my mom okay?"

"She's . . . safe, but . . ."

"What?"

"We think Vulpes has taken her back to Greenwich Park. As his prisoner."

"But why? He knows she can't help him turn back into a human."

"He hasn't kidnapped her because of that," replied Harold quietly. "He's kidnapped her because of you."

Rowan struggled to take it in, trying to work out what this all meant.

"He knows that she's the only reason you'd come back. And he needs you, Rowan. And he needs the Heart of Oak. So he can carry out his silly act of revenge in the human world. You're the only fairy who has ever become human again. It's a miracle that he'll do anything to repeat."

"But I don't know how I did it! I don't even know if the Heart of Oak had anything to do with it!"

"He won't believe you, I'm afraid," replied Harold.

"And what about the weeping beech, Harold? What about you?" said Rowan, wondering how bad this was going to get.

"We think he's destroying the trees to stop you from transforming back into a fairy—a fairy far more powerful than he is," replied Harold. "He's thinking of the prophecy. He wants to make sure that this time *he* is the fairy of most power in the Realms, and that when you come to him, it'll be as a human. He's not scared of you like that."

"Vulpes? Scared of me?" Rowan threw her head back in disbelief and stared up into the sky, watching the crows flying overhead, returning to their roosts. She could feel her eyes beginning to water.

"Were you trying to stop him, Harold?" she asked. "Is that why you look so . . . awful?"

Harold pulled himself up to his full height and ruffled his feathers, clearly a little annoyed that Rowan would think that.

"Once he'd laid waste to the beeches of Bushy Park, Olor, Aiken, Jack, and I split up to try to warn the fairies of the other parks that Vulpes was coming. Olor returned to the Fairies of the Birds in St. James's Park, Aiken went to Richmond, Jack went to the Fairies of the Beast in Regent's Park, and I came back here, and . . ."

Harold trailed off. If it hadn't been Harold, Rowan might have thought he was getting a little emotional.

"There was nothing we could do. They were too strong."

Rowan stroked his back with her finger to comfort him, but he shrugged it off.

"So we have to go and help the others," said Rowan. "And rescue my mom."

"No, it's too dangerous," replied Harold. "We worked so hard to keep you safe from Vulpes. To get you away. Your mother wouldn't want you to come back."

Rowan was a little stung by that.

"I didn't mean . . . ," said Harold quickly. "I just think she would want us to try to find other ways to help."

"So," said Rowan, composing herself again. "Any bright ideas? You know, to stop Vulpes?"

Harold looked down at Rowan's palm but didn't reply.

"We need to be doing more than just telling all the fairies that the trees are being destroyed. We need to be raising an army against Vulpes. Uniting the Realms against him."

"That's not how it works, Rowan," said Harold. "The fairies of the other Realms keep to themselves. They fear leaving their parks."

"Even if Vulpes rampages freely through them?"

"If after that he leaves them alone? Yes."

Rowan couldn't believe her ears. "Then who is going to stand up to him if I don't? Who's going to convince everyone to help us? Aiken? Crazy Jack? You?"

Rowan knew that in her frustration, she'd gone too far. She tried to soften the blow.

"We should go to the GodMother first. Ask her advice."

Harold closed his eyes. He seemed to be working everything through in his mind. "What about your dad and your sister?"

Rowan slumped a little. In her agitation she'd slightly forgotten about them. She didn't want to leave them again, but in reality how could they actually help? Her dad clearly didn't believe anything, and Willow was only nine and would just get in the way. No, she knew it was all up to her now. She might be stepping into a trap, but what choice did she have?

"ROWAN SNOWMAN!" came a shout from nearby. It was Willow looking for her.

Rowan swallowed hard. "They were okay without me before. They'll be okay again." Though in her heart of hearts it went against her every instinct to leave them.

Harold nodded his acceptance.

"IS THAT HAROLD?"

Willow suddenly appeared at Rowan's shoulder. Rowan's heart sank. This was going to make things a lot more difficult.

"Yes, Willow," said Rowan. "It's Harold."

"Oh. My. Goodness!" said a wide-eyed Willow. "SAY SOMETHING!"

Harold cocked his head at Rowan as if to ask what he should do.

"He's not a performing monkey, Willow, and we don't have time for this. The Realms are in danger, Mom is in danger, and I'm the only one who can do anything about it," said Rowan.

"I can help, Rowan. I'll come with you," said Willow.

"No, Willow. I know you mean well, but the Realms are no place for someone who's not even ten yet. It's hard enough by myself, without having to worry about you too."

"But—but I can be useful," spluttered Willow, her lip starting to wobble a little. "I do difficult things all the time."

"ROWAN!" It was Dad shouting off in the distance

now. Rowan started to fret. She couldn't waste any more time and needed to put an end to this now.

"You know what, Willow? Actually, you don't. Actually, it's me who does these difficult things. Since Mom disappeared, I'm the one who looks after Dad. And I'm the one who looks after you. And now it's up to me to bring this family back together. So the one thing that you could do for me that would be helpful is to stay out of the way and let me get on with it."

Willow blinked back a small tear. "You don't want me?"

"How many times, Willow? No. I. Don't!"

Rowan instantly regretted saying what she had, knowing that in her impatience she'd gone too far. But her pride stopped her from backing down. A large tear slipped down Willow's face as she stared back at Rowan, looking for all the world like her big sister had just torn her heart out. Rowan instinctively moved to comfort her, but Willow was having none of it. Without another word Willow dashed off.

Rowan turned to see Harold cocking his head sideways at her.

"I know, Harold. You don't have to tell me."

"ROWAN AND WILLOW!" Dad was even closer now.

"Let's get to St. James's Park, Harold. Before he finds us."

"OH MY GOD, WILLOW!" came the rather disturbed cry from Dad somewhere nearby.

Rowan looked at Harold as if to ask what on earth that could be about. She immediately worried that Willow had been hurt.

"Oh no," said Harold.

"What do you mean 'Oh no'?" said Rowan. "That doesn't sound good."

"Surely not—"

"Spit it out!"

"There's a weeping beech that Vulpes might have missed. It's only small, but . . ."

Rowan didn't need to hear any more. The sick feeling in her stomach told her what must have just happened. She crashed through the undergrowth toward the sound of her dad. Breaking out into the open, she saw him clambering gingerly out of a much smaller version of the great weeping beech that had been destroyed, this one no bigger than a small tent. He was holding something very carefully in his hands.

When he looked up to see Rowan coming toward him, she could see that his face was as white as a sheet. As she drew nearer, he slowly opened his hand, and there, in his palm, was a fairy. Except not just any fairy. It was Willow.

Chapter Three

THE BEECH WEEPS

"Look, Rowan! I'm a fairy too!" said Willow in a high-pitched, tinkly voice, stating perhaps the most obvious thing she had ever stated. She spread her arms out wide to show off her golden, oak-leaf wings.

For Rowan it was a shock, but for Dad it looked far worse.

"It can't—it can't be real," he said. "I'm dreaming, hallucinating."

Rowan took his other hand to calm him.

"No, Dad. I'm afraid it's very real."

"Does that mean, everything else you said . . ."

At that very moment Harold landed on Rowan's shoulder, seeing Willow in the palm of Dad's hand.

"Oh dear," said Harold.

"He CAN speak!" squeaked the tiny fairy Willow.

Any color remaining in Dad's cheeks drained away as he looked from his miniature daughter to the talking bird.

"*Now* what do we do?" asked Rowan, as much to herself as to Harold.

"It is what it is," said Harold. "We carry on."

"But—but we have to change her back," spluttered Dad. "How do we change her back?"

"No way!" shouted Willow. "This is amazing!"

And with that, she leapt out of her father's hand in an entirely fearless swan dive. Her wings spread wide but didn't quite catch the air properly, and she landed with an almighty *thump* on the grass. Rowan winced.

"They don't work so well when they're new," said Rowan, bending down to scoop Willow off the ground, before turning to her dad. "I'm afraid it's not so easy to turn back. I spent quite a while trying last time, and I still don't know exactly how I did it."

"But we have to do something," pleaded Dad.

"We do," said Rowan. "We have to rescue Mom. We'll just have to do it with Willow as a fairy until we work out how to change her back."

Dad went quiet for a second as he processed every-thing Rowan was saying.

"Sylvia . . . ," he murmured.

It was Rowan and Willows' mother's name. A name Rowan hadn't heard spoken out loud in many years. And certainly not by her father.

"Yes, Dad," said Rowan. "It's *all* true. She's here, in the Fairy Realms. And we're going to change her back too. But first we have to go and seek the help of the GodMother in the Park of St. James."

Dad nodded slowly, slightly in a daze.

"TO THE GODMOTHER!" squeaked Willow, who had no idea what she was talking about.

With dusk continuing to fall, they made their way out of Hyde Park following the same route Rowan had taken the last time, except now she wasn't flying on Harold's back—he was perched on her shoulder instead. Willow was tucked into her dad's shirt pocket with strict instructions to stay hidden from view. Something that she wasn't happy about at all.

They rounded Buckingham Palace and passed the Victoria Memorial with the gold-winged figure topping it. It was the place where Rowan had transformed into a white swallow after racing Aiken and Olor along the lake in St. James's Park. It all seemed like a lifetime ago now. She marveled at Willow—the same size that she had been, with the same wings she had had. And she felt a little twinge of envy. Despite all the pain that being a fairy had caused her, it didn't stop Rowan from missing how it had felt. To fly, to transform, to feel energy surge through her.

They reached the boundary of St. James's Park, a simple fence separating them from the green expanses within. The gates were closed now, as the park itself was—to humans at least. Rowan vaulted over the fence without a backward glance; she was bound by different rules now. Dad, on the other hand, was held back by the feeling that he was doing something he shouldn't. He looked left and right to check that the coast was clear, like the world's worst burglar, making it very obvious he was about to do something forbidden. He cautiously placed one foot on the bottom rung of the fence and swung his other leg over.

"OI, YOU!" shouted a portly park keeper, emerging

from a hut just inside the park. Rowan and Harold ducked behind a tree, out of sight. "Park's closed!"

Dad was stuck awkwardly astride the fence, caught red-handed.

"I—I . . ."

Rowan knew this wasn't going to go well. She knew Dad was a terrible liar, just like her.

"I left my . . . er, socks by the lake, and I just needed to go back and get them," said Dad.

Rowan looked to the sky in disbelief. Even by Dad's standards that was a terrible lie.

"But you're wearing socks," said the park keeper.

"Yes, that's right," said Dad. "But I always carry a spare pair, in case the others . . . get wet."

"I see," replied the park keeper, not believing a word. "Why don't you come back tomorrow when the park is open again, and I'll bet they'll still be here waiting for you."

"No, I really need to get them now," said Dad, throwing his remaining leg into the park. "I don't want the, er, ducks stealing them . . . for blankets."

And with that, he made a dash for it toward the tree where Rowan was hidden.

"Stop! Intruder!" yelled the park keeper, giving chase.

Dad just made it to the tree, plucked Willow out of his pocket, and thrust her into Rowan's hands, out of sight of the approaching park keeper.

"Find a way to make her human again, Rowan," he whispered. "And bring your mother home. I'll be waiting there for you all."

Before Rowan could answer him, he spun back around and put his hands into the air. Rowan shrank back behind the trunk of the tree so that she was completely hidden from view.

"It's a fair cop, guv'nor," Dad said. "I'll go quietly."

The park keeper narrowed his eyes suspiciously, breathing hard with the effort of his unexpected exertion.

"Just see that you do," said the park keeper. "And don't come back neither. I'll be watching." He pointed two fingers toward his eyes and then at Dad.

Dad trudged back off to the road, stealing a glance back at Rowan as he went. Hidden from the park keeper's view, she gave Dad a little wave and a sad smile. He winked back and turned away quickly to make sure she wasn't discovered too. And with that, Rowan was on her own again. Well, with a talking bird and a fairy sister for company.

"Are we going to be all right," began Willow, "without Dad?"

She was sitting on one of Rowan's shoulders, with Harold perched on the other as Rowan walked through the park. Rowan had been thinking exactly the same thing but didn't want to let on to Willow that she was scared. Fortunately, Harold jumped in.

"Your sister is the bravest person I know, Willow. And it usually rubs off on the rest of us. Besides, this time around she's a giant! Vulpes won't have a chance."

Rowan had to admit that it was a strange new experience seeing the Realms from this high up.

"There's that name again," said Willow. "What's a Vulpes?"

"He's the reason we need to be brave," said Rowan, realizing it was time Willow knew what lay ahead. "Vulpes is a fairy of the fox who will stop at nothing to become human again. Even if it means kidnapping our mom or . . . I don't even want to think about what else."

"Oh," Willow said. "Let's try to avoid him, then?"

"I'm afraid he and his foxes usually find me. He knows I found a way to transform back into a human, and he wants to know what it is."

"So you can just tell him and he'll leave us all alone?"

"I wish it were that simple," said Rowan. She held up her necklace to show Willow. "He thinks this is the key to becoming human again. They call it the Heart of Oak. But I don't know if it helped me change back. Mom thought it was all a myth."

"Oh," said Willow again. "So does that mean you don't know how I'm going to change back either?"

Rowan realized that Willow was going through the very same thought process that she had herself when she had become a fairy. But Rowan wasn't going to lie to her sister.

"That's where *you* have to be brave, Willow. But I managed to change back last time, and I'll do the same for you."

"Promise McCromise?"

Rowan gulped, but she put on her best courageous smile. "Promise McCromise."

That seemed to satisfy Willow, for now at least. But she also appeared to be a lot less excited about being a fairy than she had when she'd just become one.

"We're going to see the GodMother now, Willow," said Rowan, hoping that would sound more reassuring. "You'll like her."

"A fairy godmother? Can't she change me back? Like in Cinderella?" asked Willow.

"She's not that kind of fairy godmother, I'm afraid. She's a powerful fairy, but here in the Realms that just means you can transform into the creatures of your park. She uses her wisdom and power to look after all the Fairies of the Birds in the Park of St. James."

"Fairies of the Birds, Fairies of the Fox," said Willow. "What kind of fairy am I, then?"

"Each of the Royal Parks is home to a different fairy tribe, Willow. And you're the best there is. A tree fairy, like me," said Rowan. "Like I was, at least."

"Best there is?" teased Harold. "Typical Oakwing thing to say."

"And they call us Oakwings," said Rowan, ignoring the robin. "But that's just because they wish they were one too."

Harold rolled his eyes.

They reached the long lake that sits proudly in the middle of St. James's Park, and Rowan couldn't help catching her breath at the beauty of the summer's evening they were walking through. The pink hues of the sky were reflecting off the surface of the water, and it seemed incredibly peaceful. That was, until the calm was shattered by shrieks and howls in the distance.

"What on earth is that?" said Willow.

Rowan knew that sound all too well, and a little shudder ran through her at the thought of what might be happening.

"Foxes," she replied gravely.

Rowan picked up the pace, hurrying toward the noise. Rounding a corner, she saw the weeping beech overhanging the lake that they had danced beneath the first time she'd been a guest of the Fairies of the Birds. Although, that seemed like an age ago now. This time, however, it was not so welcoming a sight. Its leaves had been cruelly half-shorn from it, leaving bony, bare, armlike branches swinging to catch the three visitors as they passed through. They broke through the canopy into the space below to find leaves raining on top of them as if all of autumn had struck at once. Rowan shielded her eyes from the deluge, straining to see what was causing it, and then, to her horror, realized that there were hundreds of orange-furred fairies all over the tree. They were ripping it to shreds like a plague of locusts. Amongst the chaos, Rowan could see feathered Fairies of the Birds doing their best to fight off the Fox Fairies with sharpened sticks.

"No!" she yelled, as if the booming voice of a giant might stop the Fox Fairies in their tracks.

But it didn't. None of the Fairies of the Fox or the Birds even so much as turned to look at her, so intent were they on attacking the tree and one another. One fairy of the birds whooshed through her hair as it whizzed past. Rowan's startled gaze followed it down to another battle that was raging by the side of the lake, between foxes and swans, all ridden by their fairy masters. In truth the trumpeting swans were no match for the snapping jaws of the rusty beasts, and a squadron of feathered fairies was arrowing down from the air to do anything to distract the foxes.

Suddenly Rowan caught sight of Olor riding a swan that had a fox's jaws clamped around its neck. Without a second thought Rowan dived at the attacking fox, throwing Harold and Willow up into the air as she did so, but she struggled even to catch a hold of the beast. It wasn't like when she'd been able to transform into a fox herself to battle the animal head-on. As a human she felt slow and clumsy. She finally managed to catch its wriggling tail and pull it back. It released Olor's swan before turning on Rowan, urged on by its fairy rider. She did the best she could to kick it away as it snapped at her ankles like an angry Jack Russell.

"Rowan!" Olor shouted out a warning to her, and Rowan spun around to see another fox and its rider bounding toward a stricken Willow. Rowan had forgotten all about her sister in her determination to save Olor. Willow was frantically flapping her wings, trying to lift off, but could only buzz into the air a few centimeters before jerking back to the ground. The fox was almost on top of little Willow, and Rowan was too far away to do anything.

"Willow!" cried Rowan in despair, just as Harold swooped down to pluck her into the air and out of harm's way. Rowan had no time to breathe a sigh of relief, as the Fox Fairies had now realized that this human intruder was an enemy too. She was dive-bombed by a swarm of the rust-furred fairies, swirling around her head like angry mosquitoes. She swatted at them as well as she could, but they were so much quicker and more agile than she was. She could feel them pulling at her hair and screaming into her ears as she twisted this way and that to try to shake them off.

And then suddenly the attack was over. The Fox Fairies that had been plaguing her just let go and took to the air. The foxes on the ground around them all turned tail and fled. Then Rowan noticed that the leaves had stopped raining down from the beech. The foxes hadn't fled because they'd won; they'd fled because there were no leaves left to shred. With the tree bare, the foxes' job was done.

Chapter Four

A CURE FOR FIRE

An uneasy calm descended as the extent of the damage to tree and birds became clear. The ground was littered with leaves and feathers, and a mournful harmonic sound emanated from the wings of the Fairies of the Birds who were floating down to the ground to tend to their wounded friends.

Harold alighted back on Rowan's shoulder, with Willow riding on his back. Rowan reached out a protective hand to enfold them both—it was the closest she could manage to a hug, and it felt wholly inadequate after Willow's brush with the jaws of the fox.

"Thank you for saving my sister, Harold," said Rowan.

"Don't worry. I'm well practiced in rescuing you girls from the foxes," he replied.

Rowan cracked a small smile. He'd done pretty much exactly the same thing when she'd first become a fairy.

"Hey, Oakwing!" came a shout from the ground below. It was Olor. Rowan crouched down and held out her hand. Olor jumped into her palm and looked up into Rowan's huge face. "I'm glad you came back. And I imagine she will be too."

Olor pointed behind Rowan's head, and she turned to see what her feathered fairy friend was looking at. On the lake a brown duck swam toward them, surrounded by a flotilla of downy chicks that she'd obviously been caring for during the battle. In one swift movement the duck seemed to lift out of the water, spin, and continue onto the land, now striding forward as a fairy with a great flowing robe.

"Wow," whispered Willow from Rowan's shoulder. "Who is *that*?"

"GodMother!" cried Rowan.

The GodMother nodded her head in acknowledgment and sprang into the air to hover in front of their faces.

"I'm sorry we couldn't be here sooner, GodMother," said Rowan.

"You have no need to apologize, child," the God-Mother replied. "It's Vulpes's madness we have to thank for this."

"Then we must find him and fight fire with fire," said Rowan firmly.

The GodMother inclined her head to one side and looked at Rowan quizzically.

"I find that the best cure for fire is water."

Rowan shrank back, a little chastened. She felt Olor reach out to hold her thumb in reassurance.

"But one thing is clear," the GodMother continued. "We will have to work together to stop him. It won't be any easier with you as a human, Rowan, but I see you brought a little help with you," she said, looking at Willow.

Willow wasn't sure what to do, so did a little curtsy, which made the GodMother smile.

At that moment a bird swooped under the tree above their heads, and a tiny fairy figure jumped off and floated to the ground like a parachutist jumping from a plane. He wore clothes made of rusty brown leaves, with bark for armor, and had a belt around his body with sharp sticks tucked into it.

"Did you miss me?" the fairy asked, landing squarely on the earth with his two hands on his hips, ready for action.

"Of course, Aiken," said Rowan with a smile.

"Have you been away?" muttered Harold under his breath.

"As you know, beak face," said Aiken, "I've been to Richmond to see the Fairies of the Deer. But I wasn't expecting to see *you* when I got back!"

He slapped Rowan's foot with his hand like he was giving it a high five.

"What happened, Aiken?" said Harold a little impatiently.

"Keep your feathers on, Harold. I was getting to that," said Aiken. "The Fox Fairies had already destroyed the beech of Richmond Park before I got there."

"Will the deer help us against Vulpes?" asked Rowan.

"Why would they do that?" replied Aiken. "They think it's all about you and him. What happened with our friends the Tree Fairies, Harold?"

Harold looked at the ground.

"Ah, well, no surprise there," said Aiken.

"What can we do, GodMother?" asked Rowan.

"You will need all the help you can get if you're to fight off hordes of foxes and rescue your mother. More than our birds can give you. You'll need to convince Simeon to lend you the strength of the Beast of Regent's Park."

"Simeon?" asked Rowan.

"He is the one they look to for guidance in Regent's Park," replied the GodMother. "But he will see no reason to come to your aid."

"Why not?" asked Rowan.

"Because there's very little that he cares about," replied the GodMother. "But if you understand what those things are, you may have a chance."

Rowan waited expectantly for her to explain, but she didn't.

"What about Jack?" asked Rowan.

"You know Jack Pike by now," said the GodMother. "You'd just better hope he hasn't made things more difficult for you with Simeon."

"We must go, then," said Rowan.

The GodMother nodded.

"Who's Jack Pike?" Willow asked.

"Fairy of the river," Aiken replied. "Likes your mom. A bit too much. Slippery bloke in all kinds of ways."

Rowan looked to Olor.

"Are you able to join us?"

Olor launched into the air, but her wings made a discordant sound as she did so. She grimaced.

"I must have damaged them in the battle," she said, jerking sideways as if she didn't have total control over them. She fell awkwardly, and Aiken caught her in his arms.

The GodMother took Olor's wings in her hands and ran her fingers carefully through the feathers. Tiny plumes were coming away and falling to the ground. The GodMother spread her own wings out behind her and, after pointing one forward, gracefully combed her fingers between the feathers. The same sorry shower spiraled to the ground. Next she passed to Willow and repeated the motion, but the waxy oak leaves that formed her wings seemed to stick firm.

The GodMother turned to Harold. "Did Vulpes leave any weeping beeches in Hyde Park intact?"

"A small one, yes. Where Willow fell in as a fairy."

"I see. Then this is more serious than I'd feared."

"What's happening, GodMother?" asked Rowan.

"I can't be certain," she replied, "but my worry is that the destruction of the weeping beeches is taking its toll on us. We know the trees are our portals into this world, and they have a power we don't fully understand. But we are deeply connected with them. Destroying them would not only take away the means of *becoming* a fairy; I suspect it would also begin to take away what makes us a fairy once we are here. That's why your wings are beginning to fail, Olor."

Olor looked horrified.

"But what about Willow and Aiken? Why aren't they suffering it too?" asked Rowan.

"I believe it is because Vulpes missed a tree in Hyde Park. There should be only one portal in every Royal Park, but you found the exception. So there is still a source of energy for the Fairies of the Trees."

"Does Vulpes know what he's doing?" asked Rowan.

"Perhaps," replied the GodMother. "But no one fully understands the balance of energy and power in the Realms. All we know is that it is fragile."

"So what happens if he destroys all the trees? Is there anything we can do to save them?" asked Rowan.

"I remember, during the Second World War, the German bombs rained on the parks, and we lost many trees and many fairies. The Queen arranged for the survivors to be secretly evacuated to the countryside, where they were able to form a connection to other beeches, until the ones in the parks grew back," said the GodMother.

"How long did they take to grow back?" asked Rowan, alarmed.

"Until they were mature enough to provide a source of energy to a fairy?" said the GodMother. "About twenty years."

"Then stopping Vulpes is even more important than we thought," said Rowan. "Harold, Aiken. Let's go and find Jack at Regent's Park. We're going to need the help of as many beasts as we can find."

"I'm coming too," said Olor.

"And what about me?" said Willow.

"Olor, you're weak from this sickness, and we don't know if it's going to get worse," said Rowan. "And

Willow, you're safer here with the GodMother. She will look after you until I can come back."

"I don't want to lie here and wait for something terrible to happen to me, Rowan," said Olor. "And you'll need all the help you can get against Vulpes."

"I can help too, Rowan!" said Willow, putting up her fists in an unconvincing show of strength.

"Willow, you don't even know how to use your wings properly yet."

Willow's face fell. Olor flew awkwardly to put her arm around Willow. "I will teach her."

Rowan slumped to the ground, and the others gathered at her feet. "It's okay for you, Olor. She's not your sister. You're not responsible for what happens to her. How can I look after her, and you, and stop Vulpes? And all with these great lumbering arms and legs, and none of the powers I had as a fairy? When I was a fairy, I could change form. I had control over nature! Some of the time, at least. . . ."

"There is one way to get your powers back," said the GodMother.

Rowan stopped in her tracks as she realized what the GodMother was suggesting.

"You mean become a fairy again?" said Rowan. "What if I don't find the way back to being human like I did before?"

"You said we'd find a way!" said Willow, clearly upset at the thought that they might not.

Rowan felt awful that she'd scared Willow again. Rescuing Mom was never going to be easy, but it seemed to be getting more difficult by the second. Her head was full of thoughts all pulling in opposite directions.

"I don't like saying it," said the GodMother. "I know it's a risk."

"But I don't even know if I can change back into a fairy. How am I supposed to weep beneath the beech tree now that I know there are people who love me?"

"Just remember that the most potent tears," replied the GodMother, "are the ones shed for others and not for yourself."

Rowan wasn't quite sure what that meant, but she knew now that becoming a fairy again was her only option.

"We need Rowan Oakwing back," pleaded Aiken.

Rowan looked around at the little faces in front of her, and finally to Harold.

"It is what it is, right?" she said to him.

He nodded slowly, clearing away any lasting doubts in Rowan's mind.

"Okay, then we need to get to the weeping beech in Regent's Park before Vulpes does."

Rowan turned to the GodMother, an idea forming in her head.

"GodMother, will Cervus and the Fairies of the Deer listen to you?" asked Rowan. "Would Sylvan and the Fairies of the Trees?"

"Perhaps," she replied.

"Could you plead our case to them? Get them to join us?"

The GodMother nodded. "I will see you at dawn, at the gates of Greenwich Park, with whatever help I have been able to muster. You should bring all the help you can too," she said, motioning toward Olor and Willow.

Rowan bowed her head in acceptance, though she felt a little sick to her stomach too. It was about far more than just her now. There was not going to be any running away from Vulpes this time. On the contrary, she was going to have to run toward him as quickly as she could.

✴ Chapter Five ✴
THE RETURN OF ROWAN OAKWING

Rowan picked her way carefully down a tree-lined path through Regent's Park, looking left and right to make sure any patrolling park keepers didn't throw them out. She was lucky enough as it was to have sneaked in as the last light of the evening was fading, with a robin perched on one shoulder and Willow, Aiken, and Olor stowed in her pockets.

"Where does this Simeon live, Harold?" asked Rowan. "In a tree? By a lake?"

"He lives with the beasts," replied Harold.

"What does that mean?" asked Willow.

"In London Zoo," replied Harold.

Rowan's eyes widened, and she gulped slightly. She

didn't like to think what a "beast" could do to them. She hoped they wouldn't have to get close enough to find out. She could feel Olor and Aiken wriggling in one of her pockets, jammed up against each other.

"All right in there, you two?" asked Rowan.

"I would be if Aiken weren't taking up all the space," said Olor.

"Don't get your feathers in a crease," replied Aiken. "Plenty of room for both of us."

They soon reached the gates of the zoo, where security guards were manning the entrance. It was nothing fancy—it could have been the entrance to a school—but there was clearly no way through. Rowan ducked back out of sight.

"We need to fly over the back fence," said Harold. "We need to get to the beech before Vulpes does."

"Let's go," said Rowan. "Lead the way."

Harold leapt off her shoulder and swooped away into the darkness. Rowan hurried after him around the back of the zoo. They soon reached a tree standing by itself within sight of the zoo's protective railings. It was a weeping beech, and its leaves were still intact, rustling gently in the breeze. Rowan breathed a sigh of relief.

"It's time to change now, Rowan."

Rowan was still struggling with the idea. She knew it was the right thing to do, and part of her was even looking forward to feeling the wings on her back again, but she also knew the perils of being a fairy now. And she knew how hard it had been last time to get back to being a human again. She looked down at Willow, sitting in her top pocket, her tiny face turned up toward hers, and Rowan knew she had to do it for Willow.

"Quickly now, Rowan," said Harold. "We can't have more than a few minutes of dusk left."

Olor and Aiken spilled gratefully out of Rowan's pocket to buzz in the air beside her, but Willow didn't seem to want to leave the safety of her shirt. She was clinging on to her pocket like a seasick passenger gripping the rail of a ship.

"Can't I stay with you?" asked Willow.

Rowan shook her head. "You'll be just fine with my friends, Willow. And I need to do this alone."

Rowan plucked a reluctant Willow out of her shirt and placed her carefully onto the grass. Harold, Aiken, and Olor alighted next to Willow to make sure she was okay.

"What's that noise?" asked Willow.

And just as she said it, Rowan could hear it too. A low hum, off in the distant gloom. They all turned their heads toward the sound. It was getting louder, and closer.

"The Fairies of the Fox," said Harold. "They're coming."

Aiken pulled two sticks out of his belt. "I'm ready."

Olor grabbed Willow and sprang into the air. "There're too many of them. We have to hide."

"Olor's right," said Harold. "You have to be quick, Rowan. We can't hold them off."

Rowan squinted her eyes to stare into the distance. She could see them now. Like a flock of starlings, the Fairies of the Fox seemed to swarm in the sky, while beneath them a skulk of foxes was breaking through the undergrowth and into the open, following their fairy masters.

"Now, Rowan," said Harold. "Run!"

Rowan needed no second bidding. As her friends took off to the safety of a nearby oak tree, she rushed under the canopy of the great beech and crashed breathlessly to the ground with her back to the trunk.

It's time to cry, she thought. *Time to cry.* But where were the tears going to come from to make the magic work this time? She screwed her eyes tight shut and willed the weeping to start, but she could feel nothing coming. And she could hear the Fox Fairies getting closer outside. The low hum had turned into the symphonic sound of a hundred violins that the fairies' wings made when they vibrated in unison. Rowan bit into her hand to try to make the pain force out the tears. Her eyes began to water, and she bit down harder. A drop squeezed out of the corner of her eye and landed on the bark. Was it enough? Still nothing. She could hear the pounding of the foxes' paws on the grass now too. How could she hold off a whole mob of foxes all by herself?

She tried to brush the mess of thoughts into the corners of her mind, to clear a space to think. *Concentrate, Rowan,* she told herself. *It's not tears of pain; it's the tears of the unloved that cause the transformation.* She thought about how she'd felt the first time she'd become a fairy beneath the beech in Hyde Park. The way she had been missing her mom so much. The way she'd felt that her dad just didn't care. But now she knew her mom hadn't disappeared forever, that her dad did love her.

Thwack! High above her something had hit the tree. *Thwack! Thwack!* And now more. Rowan looked up to see leaves spiraling down. *Thwack! Thwack! Thwack!* It was happening all around her now. The Fairies of the Fox were swarming around the tree, plucking the leaves from the beech, causing shafts of moonlight to break through and strike the trunk. Rowan shrank back against the tree. Were the foxes on the ground going to rush in and attack? She could see dark shapes silhouetted through the branches. The foxes were patrolling outside but clearly didn't know she was there. The tree was hiding her from them. For now, at least. *Thwack! Thwack! Thwack! Thwack!* The leaves were raining down all around her.

And then they came back to her, the words the GodMother had said. "The most potent tears are the ones shed for others and not for yourself." Rowan thought of all the children out in the city right now who felt they had nowhere to turn, who felt that no one cared. Just like she had felt. And she thought of them coming to the park to escape from their lives just for a moment, and seeing the weeping beeches like great skeletons against the sky, with no hope of refuge beneath their branches and no chance of entering this magical Realm, with all the joy and excitement it offered. She thought of what might happen to children like Aiken if they never had the opportunity to be something else, or people like her mother if the sadness were just too much for them to bear.

A feeling rose up inside her like the swell of the sea. *Thwack!* The leaves kept dropping. She felt her breath catch, her rib cage shudder, and her mouth go dry. *Thwack! Thwack!* Her bottom lip stiffened, and she could feel her eyes filling with tears. *Thwack! Thwack! Thwack!* The first teardrop broke free of her eye and ran down her cheek before splashing onto the bark of the tree. Arrows of light pierced the beech from top to bottom now. Fairies of the Fox were inside the canopy above her, attacking it from both inside and out. Rowan raised her head to look at them, with tears streaming down her face. Both tree and human were now weeping in unison, but while the leaves fell to the ground, the tiny droplets of sadness fell onto the bark. Rowan looked down to see them seeping into the heart of the ancient tree.

"It's her!" yelled one of the Fairies of the Fox. They had been so intent on destroying the tree, they hadn't noticed the human sitting at the foot of it. Until now. Rowan saw the silhouettes outside the canopy of the tree raise their heads. The foxes knew something was wrong. A furred, orange head broke through the branches to see why the fairies were shouting. Its eyes opened wide at the sight of Rowan, and it yelped a warning. Rowan felt caught like a deer on the road at night, not knowing which way to run. Had the magic worked? Had her tears found their mark?

As the pack of foxes broke through the leaves, a new sensation came upon her. Not sadness this time but *transformation*. Rowan felt her chest tightening and a feeling in her heart like it was shrinking and drawing all the other organs in her body toward it. Her whole form was being sucked into a smaller and smaller space, and as everything else pulled in, she felt those familiar wings pushing out of her back. It was as if they had never been away. The muscles were tingling the way an asleep leg does as the feeling comes back into it. The foxes looked on in awe, transfixed by the sight of a human becoming a fairy. Rowan stretched out her wings as far as they would reach and beat them hard to bring the muscles back to life. She knew she had only a moment before the foxes remembered they had the upper hand. There were a lot of them, against only one tiny fairy. She needed to even up the odds, but could she transform again so soon? Would she still have control over her transformations like she'd had just before she'd become human again?

Rowan vaulted into the air, trying to clear her mind. She knew that concentration was the best chance she had of convincing her body to respond to her mind's instructions. That was the lesson she'd learned fighting against Vulpes and his foxes the first time. She spun in the air, visualizing herself as the great white fox. Once again she felt her muscles contract, but this time her limbs extended and contorted. She crashed back to the ground as a snarling white fox. The orange furred beasts surrounding her shrank back in shock once again. She took advantage of their fear, bounding at them and howling right in their muzzles. One or two ran away immediately. Other, braver ones stood their ground, and then sprang to attack. She scratched and bit as well as she could, wrestling and rolling her foes through the falling leaves, only for them to return again and again. Still she fought, but there was nothing to gain but survival. Above her head the tree was now practically bare. And then, just as they had at St. James's, the foxes suddenly turned tail and ran, their work done. The Fairies of the Fox followed them by air, then descended to land on the backs of their animal friends, to be carried out of the park and back to Greenwich, no doubt.

Rowan emerged from beneath the skeletal branches, shaking, and shrinking back into a battered and bruised fairy form.

"Rowan!" shouted Willow from Harold's back, as she and Rowan's friends flew down from their hiding place. "Are you okay?"

"Never better," said Rowan, still flushed red with the sweat of combat, and wincing from the pain of her injuries.

Willow gave her an enormous hug. "It's good to be the same size again."

Rowan managed a little smile. In a way, it was.

"Welcome back, Rowan Oakwing," said Harold. "We've got a lot to do."

✳ Chapter Six ✳
THE FAIRIES OF THE BEAST

"Are we ready to fly?" asked Harold. "Simeon and the Fairies of the Beast are just through there," he said, pointing over a high fence into the shadowy London Zoo behind them.

"How are you feeling, Olor?" Rowan asked her friend.

Olor beat her wings, wincing a little as she did so.

"Compared to what you've just gone through," said Olor, "I'm sure I'll be fine."

Willow buzzed her wings and immediately fell flat on her face.

"I don't think you're ready to fly solo just yet," said Harold. "Climb on." He held out a wing for her.

"Let's go!" shouted Aiken, launching himself skyward.

As they lifted up over the fence, a roar pierced the air.

"What's that?" asked Willow.

"Not a fox," replied Harold.

Their faces fell.

Inside the nighttime zoo it was even eerier than it had been out in the park. By day you could pretend that the humans were in charge, but in the dark it felt like the animals ruled the roost. Rowan couldn't see much, but she could smell a great deal, and hear a lot more. As they passed the enclosures, growls and howls grated the air, making the fairies all shudder with wondering what could be making the sounds.

And then the scariest noises yet rang out from somewhere in the blackness. It started with heavy breathing, became a bark, and then turned into a howl. But what was making the sound didn't seem like a fox, or even a dog. It sounded much, much bigger than that. And clearly whatever it was, was very excited, or angry, about something.

"Gorillas," Harold confirmed.

They sailed over the top of some waving bamboo to land on a branch, and saw what looked like a vast island emerging out of the darkness in front of them. On one side were gigantic, glass-fronted buildings that enabled human visitors to get close to the beasts without endangering themselves. Low-lit paths went in and out of the buildings and were protected by fences and then a broad moat of water. The animals were clearly far too dangerous to be allowed anywhere near human beings. In the middle of the island, great wooden structures made of felled trees with rope strung between them created a giant jungle gym. And when Rowan saw that, she started to make out the source of the commotion. Right in the middle of the wooden construction was gathered a small troop of immense gorillas. They were making a ferocious din, but even despite that, Rowan could hear a familiar voice ringing out. It was Jack.

"Jack's in there!" Rowan whispered urgently.

"I know," replied Harold. "That's where Simeon lives."

Rowan's heart sank.

"Right. Of course. The leader of the Fairies of the

Beast would live on a pitch-black island surrounded by huge, scary animals," said Rowan.

"It is what it is," replied Harold.

Rowan shot him a look. "I thought we'd finished with that."

Harold shrugged his wings.

"Okay, everyone ready?" said Rowan.

"Er . . ." Aiken didn't seem so sure.

Rowan took a deep breath. "They're just big, cuddly monkeys. Let's go!"

They sprang off the branch and over the moat . . . toward the gorillas. They landed on a rope that was close enough to see the small band of them, but for the moment at least, the fairies were just out of reach. In the middle of the gathering, Rowan could see what was holding the gorillas' attention. An awesomely large silverback was dangling something between its fingers and batting it back and forth like a baby with a new toy. The toy was a rather dizzy-looking Jack Pike. Nestled above the gorillas in the crook of a tree lay a fairy with black fur robes and a dramatic silver stripe streaked over his head. He was the largest fairy Rowan had seen yet, both in height and in breadth, and he seemed to be a little bored with the show. A horde of Fairies of the Beast wearing fur-trimmed clothes in all manner of colors buzzed around him, attending to his every need. Then the silver-striped fairy spoke to Jack in an extremely proper, incredibly elegant accent. It could only be Simeon.

"Now, for the last time. Are you going to say sorry?" he said.

Jack looked up at him. However long he'd been here, he clearly hadn't been having too much fun.

"But there's nothing to apologize for," replied Jack stubbornly.

Simeon gestured to the gorillas. "These magnificent beasts are very sensitive. You can't just barge in here like you own the place. It disturbs their natural routine."

"I am the King of the Fairies of the River!" announced Jack.

"Is he?" whispered Willow to Rowan in their hiding place.

But Rowan didn't hear her. She was listening as hard as she could to Simeon.

"He thinks he is," offered Harold instead.

"All the more reason to set an example," said Simeon.

"This is outrageous!" screamed Jack.

"Throw him to the tigers," Simeon replied casually with a dismissive flick of his hand.

"Stop!" shouted Rowan.

All eyes swiveled to stare at Rowan. Rowan suddenly didn't feel quite so brave.

"Another intruder!" said Simeon.

Rowan held down her nerves and hovered up in the air, but her wings told a different story, as the music they made seemed quite off-key. She floated down to the ground to land in front of the assembled watchers.

"Rowan Oakwing," said Jack. "Surprised to see you, but not complaining."

Rowan smiled awkwardly. She couldn't quite believe she was risking life and limb for someone as untrustworthy as Jack Pike.

"I'm very sorry to interrupt," said Rowan, "but we've come to ask a very important favor."

"A favor! While I'm trying to make an example of this extremely rude fairy here?" yelled Simeon.

Rowan thought fast. "Er, yes. It's just that me and

my friends here"—she gestured back to Harold, Olor, Aiken, and Willow—"we were very keen to . . . *watch*."

"What?" blurted Jack.

"Fairies who disrespect their animal friends should really be punished," continued Rowan.

Simeon thought for a second.

"You're right," he said. "And seeing as you have already apologized, I am prepared to overlook the fact that you too have arrived here without a formal invitation."

Rowan beckoned the others down. They also looked at her as if they had no idea what she was doing. Which they clearly didn't.

"Wonderful," said Simeon. "To the tiger enclosure!"

"No!" shouted Jack.

"Before we do," said Rowan as quickly and as bravely as she could. "The gorillas. What are their names?"

Simeon looked at Rowan quizzically.

"The names the humans have given them?" he replied. "Or the ones I have?"

Rowan sensed she was onto something.

"The ones you have, of course," she said.

Simeon pointed to the large silverback that was still holding Jack.

"That is Mateso." He turned to a smaller ape. "That is Upweke." Then he pointed to a baby. "And that little one is Kukata Tamaa." He seemed to fall into a little reverie as he spoke their names, but he soon snapped out of it. "Anyway. To the tigers!"

"What language are the words from?" said Rowan, stalling again.

Simeon was getting a little exasperated now.

"It's Swahili. The language of East Africa. The home of the great apes. But we don't have any more time to—"

"What do the words mean?"

Simeon's exasperation moved to annoyance. He flew straight over to Rowan and stood far too close, staring her right in the eyes as if he could see all the way to the back of her head.

"You ask a lot of questions," he said quietly. "Why shouldn't we throw you to the tigers as well?"

Rowan's legs started to shake.

"They're beautiful names. For beautiful animals. I just wanted to know more about them," said Rowan, trying not to show her fear.

Simeon remained expressionless. Rowan wondered

if he was about to attack, but she held her nerve. After what seemed an age, he slowly began to speak. Very quietly.

"'Mateso.' It means 'suffering.' 'Upweke' means 'loneliness.'" Rowan was so close to Simeon, she could see a small tear slip out of his eye. "And 'Kukata Tamaa' means 'hopelessness.'"

Rowan tentatively put out a hand but wasn't yet brave enough to comfort him.

"Why did you give them those names, Simeon?" asked Rowan.

He seemed to relax a little, but he was still suspicious.

"Why should I tell you?"

"You don't have to," said Rowan. "But if it's difficult for you to say, it must be important."

He narrowed his eyes, but she sensed that he might trust her.

"When I was a young boy," he began slowly, "my father took my mother and me on a business trip to Africa. It was the only time he ever took us away with him. He was rich and powerful and he didn't like anyone. Not my mother, and certainly not me. While he was working, my mother and I went to see gorillas in the wild. It was the most beautiful thing we'd ever seen. We were so happy. When we got home, he sent me to boarding school far, far away. And he stopped my mother from ever coming to see me."

Rowan felt a lump come up in her throat. "How did you fall into the Realms?" she asked.

"I became obsessed with Africa. I read all the books I could find in our school library. One day we were on a school trip, to London Zoo. And there was a famous gorilla living here. I couldn't tear my eyes away from him. He seemed sad and trapped here, like me. So I hid myself away from the rest of the group and stayed after dusk. I fell asleep under a beech tree, and woke up . . . as a fairy."

"And you haven't seen your mother since?" asked Rowan.

"No," said Simeon softly. "These animals have cared for me instead. And I care for them. But I gave them their names to remind me of her."

Rowan rested her hand on his shoulder to reassure him.

"I know how you feel, Simeon," said Rowan. "I

know what it feels like to think you're never going to see your mother again."

Rowan told him her sorry tale in exchange for the one she had just heard. He was gripped and saddened almost as much at hearing Rowan's story as he had been by his own. When she'd come to an end, he reached out and laid his hand on her arm to comfort her, as she had done. A bond had been made.

"What is the favor you came here to ask?" he said.

"We need help to stop Vulpes and to rescue my mother."

Simeon nodded. "What can I do?"

"Could we perhaps borrow him?" She pointed at Jack, who smiled hopefully back.

"If this fairy is useful to you, he's certainly no use to me," said Simeon. "Is that all you want?"

"We need the help of the beasts," said Rowan. "We're not strong enough to fight Vulpes on our own. Will you join us?"

Simeon considered this for a moment before shaking his head.

"I haven't left this park in many years. The outside world has not been kind to me. I prefer to stay."

Rowan was downcast. "How—"

"But I have a suggestion," Simeon interrupted. "Take one animal each. Any more, and you won't control them. If you can break them out, of course. The human zoo-keepers here have them well locked in. Choose wisely."

"Thank you, Simeon," said Rowan, although she had no idea what they were going to do.

"Then, when you have your beasts," continued Simeon, "the easiest way to Greenwich without attracting attention will be on the canal that runs through the zoo. Find a boat, and it should take you all the way to the Thames."

Rowan nodded her thanks again and turned to Jack, who bolted forward to join her before Simeon changed his mind. Sharing relieved looks, the fairies all flew off the island and out into the zoo.

Before very long they were all standing by a long, glass-walled enclosure.

"Is this the animal you want, Rowan?" asked Aiken.

"What is it?" asked Willow.

"There's a sign here," said Olor.

"*Panthera tigris*. Habitat: tropical rain forest," read Harold. "It's a—"

But before he could say the word, they all heard a deep growl reverberate behind the glass.

"Tiger," said Rowan.

"Couldn't we get a rabbit instead?" said Willow.

"That wouldn't really help us defeat Vulpes, Willow," replied Rowan.

"How are we ever going to get it out?" asked Aiken.

Just then they heard human footsteps. They hid behind a bulletin board as a security guard appeared, and they watched her follow the glass wall along to a door marked "Staff Only." Without a second thought Rowan sprang high into the air to hover above the security guard's head. Her wings made that familiar harmonic sound, but she couldn't stop them. The guard looked this way and that, convinced she could hear something, it seemed. Rowan watched her punch a number code into a lock on the door and walk in. Rowan tried to follow, but she was too slow, and the door slammed in her face. *Oh nine oh four,* she thought. *Oh nine oh four.* She hovered down to the keypad and pushed at the buttons with all her might, but it was no good. Her fairy fingers just weren't strong enough. She was soon joined by Aiken and Olor, both lending their weight, but there was no way they could manage it. They crashed to the floor, defeated.

"Not as easy as it looks here, is it?" said Jack somewhat sarcastically.

"It would be easier if you helped, fin face," said Aiken.

"Stop it, boys," said Rowan, trying to think while out of breath from all the heaving. If only she had her human fingers back for a moment. Then she had an idea. She flew up into the air and tried to clear her mind as she began to spin.

"Who are you calling 'fin face,' Oakwing?" said Jack to Aiken, breaking Rowan's concentration.

"Shhh," said Harold. "Rowan needs some quiet."

"Slime-licker," muttered Aiken under his breath.

"Go away!" snapped Harold. "Both of you!" Which wiped the smile off Jack's face. "Make yourselves useful and go find your own animals," Harold finished.

Aiken and Jack moped off. If they'd had tails, they would have carried them between their legs right now.

"Sorry, Rowan," said Harold. "Please continue."

"You can do it, Rowan!" said Willow. "You always do!"

Rowan started again, feeling the weight of responsibility building. She tried to visualize an animal with fingers like a human. A gorilla! But for some reason the transformation wasn't happening. Maybe because her concentration had been broken? She fluttered back to the ground and landed forlornly in a heap.

"I can't do it," she said. "I don't know why."

"It's okay," said Olor, trying to reassure her. "It'll come back."

Minutes passed, but it seemed like hours to Rowan before a voice came out of the darkness.

"Don't worry, everyone. I've got this."

It was Aiken, springing forward into the light, riding on the back of a bright-eyed, live-wire squirrel monkey.

Harold raised his eyes to the heavens.

"This is my new friend," said Aiken. "I call him 'Fingers.'"

* Chapter Seven *
THE GREAT ESCAPE

The lights of the city seemed to sparkle far from Greenwich Park, the place where Sylvia, Rowan's mother, was looking out from atop a gnarled old tree. Gazing out over London used to bring her such comfort, but now it only filled her with trepidation and fear for what might be happening out there. She stretched her arms out in the air as if to try to reach her family, her wings straining against the bonds that were tying them tightly to her back to prevent her from escaping. Next to her a familiar bitter-chocolate voice spoke quietly into her ear.

"Don't worry," whispered Vulpes. "She will come for you. She can't not."

"I hope she's in bed at home," replied Sylvia. "Sleeping through this whole thing."

Just then a fairy riding a fox appeared at the bottom of the tree. He spoke breathlessly, as if he'd just run all the way from the other side of London himself.

"Our foxes have sighted Rowan in Regent's Park," he panted. "She was a . . ." He trailed off nervously.

"Spit it out!" barked Vulpes.

"She was a fairy." He cringed.

"I'm not sure I heard you correctly," replied Vulpes. "Come closer." The hapless fairy climbed off his steed and hovered up to where Vulpes and Sylvia were perched. Vulpes spoke with quiet menace. "Tell me again."

The fox fairy looked at his feet. "She was a fairy, sir."

Vulpes seemed to suck in all the air around them, before expelling it in a ferocious blast that almost blew the fairy back out of the tree.

"HOW IS THAT POSSIBLE?" Vulpes yelled right in his face.

"I'm—I'm afraid I don't know. We destroyed all the beeches like you said—"

"Did you? DID YOU? Then explain how *the one thing* I asked you to prevent has happened?"

The fairy looked down again. Sylvia couldn't stop a small smile from creeping across her face, her concern for Rowan momentarily outweighed by the pleasure of seeing Vulpes so annoyed.

"There's something else," mumbled the fairy. "There was a new fairy . . . hiding in the trees. She looked just like her . . . like she was family."

Sylvia's heart sank again. She feared what this might mean.

Vulpes raised an eyebrow. "So not only have you failed to prevent Rowan Oakwing from becoming a fairy again, but you have now allowed her sister to become one too?"

"I can't be sure, sir."

"No, of course. You can't be sure of anything, can you?" And with that, Vulpes kicked the poor fairy square in the chest, propelling him straight out of the tree. He fell to the ground with a *thump*, unable to spread his wings quickly enough. Vulpes turned to Sylvia.

"No matter," he said calmly. "Now Rowan has *two* weaknesses in the Realms. A mother *and* a sister. I shall just have to exploit them both."

"What was the code again, Rowan?" Aiken was hovering in the air next to the lock on the door marked

"Staff Only." The nimble, yellow squirrel monkey was standing on the handle with its hand poised over the number buttons.

"Oh nine oh four," said Rowan.

Aiken whispered into the monkey's ear.

"No way," said Willow to Rowan. "Can fairies really talk to animals?"

"There's a special relationship between them," replied Rowan.

"So I could talk to them too?" said Willow, clearly blown away by the whole idea.

"We all can," said Rowan.

Aiken leaned back to give the monkey some room.

"Off you go, Fingers," he said.

And with that, Fingers started head-butting the numbers in what looked like an entirely random order.

Harold shook his head in disbelief. "Although, it doesn't mean the animal will always understand what you say."

Willow flew over to the keypad and pointed carefully at the zero, the nine, the zero again, and the four. "Like this, Fingers," she said, repeating the maneuver again and again to make sure the monkey could see. Fingers cackled and started banging out the same combination with his fists until a light flashed green and the door clicked open.

"Good work, Pillow," said Rowan as they squeezed through the gap to enter. Willow beamed proudly in response.

They made their way carefully through a concrete-floored storage area, the tiger enclosure still glass-walled to their left. But this time there was a door in the wall. The squirrel monkey swung off the handle, but the door was stuck fast.

"There's another lock," said Rowan, pointing at a black plastic box by the side of the door with a red light illuminated on it. "We'll need a security pass."

Just then there was the sound of a handle turning. The guard was coming back through the room from an office at the other end. The fairies all raced for cover. It was easy for them to shoot up to the ceiling, but the monkey just managed to scamper behind a pile of boxes in time. As the keeper left by the door they'd come in, Rowan flung herself at the door to the office before it clanged shut, managing to leave it slightly ajar. Inside the office, Rowan scanned the shelves and the walls before her eyes came to rest on a bundle of security passes hanging from a hook on the far wall.

"Bingo," she said.

Rowan flew over, but the pass was too heavy to lift. Willow joined her to help, and together they carried it back to the door to the tiger enclosure like two house movers shifting a table. As they held it over the black box to trigger the mechanism, Willow paused a moment.

"I'm just checking," said Willow, "but this is a special kind of fairy tiger too, right? The kind that does what you say, not the kind that eats you?"

"Special relationship, remember," said Rowan. "We look after them, and they look after us."

"Okay, great," said Willow, holding the pass to the box. The box light clicked green, the door opened, and Fingers sprang through.

"Not sure what they think of monkeys, though . . . ," said Harold.

"What?" cried Aiken. "Fingers!" Aiken chased after the tiny monkey, and the rest of them followed through the door.

It was dark and eerie in the enclosure, and all

Rowan could hear was the quiet harmonies of the fairies' wings as they flew onward. Aiken had found Fingers and was riding on his back as he swung through a nearby tree.

"Maybe it's gone to sleep?" asked Aiken, looking slightly seasick from the swinging.

A deep, low growl echoed out into the night. It sounded like a tractor starting up.

"Nice kitty," said Olor as two fierce orange eyes pierced the blackness in front of them.

"I think I'd rather take my chances with the foxes," said Aiken.

At that moment the tiger spotted Fingers, pinned its ears back, opened its jaws wide, and roared so hard that it made their wings all vibrate by themselves. Rowan looked at Harold as if to ask what they should do now.

"Show it you're not afraid, Rowan," said Harold. "That you are a friend."

Rowan swallowed hard. She flew cautiously forward to hover close to the tiger's face. The tiger didn't take its eyes off her. Rowan turned back to look at the rest of the group for a bit of reassurance.

The tiger roared again, taking a step forward and throwing out a paw at Rowan like a cat might bat at a ball of yarn. It knocked Rowan to the ground and stood over her, growling. Rowan lifted her head slowly to see her friends' looks of concern.

"Don't look a tiger in the eye," whispered Harold. "And whatever you do, don't turn your back."

"Now you tell me," hissed Rowan.

Harold shrugged an apology. Rowan sat up and faced the tiger again, feeling the hair-dryer heat of its breath on her body.

"Is there anything that scares *them*?" asked Rowan without turning around this time.

"What did they do in *The Jungle Book*?" Willow piped up.

As silly as it may have sounded, it gave Rowan an idea. What had Jack told her back in Bushy Park? That she might have the power to control nature itself? It had worked with water when she was fighting Vulpes. Might it work again? The only other thing she knew for sure was that her powers didn't always seem to work when she wanted them to. . . .

She dragged herself to her feet, cleared her mind,

and rose to float in the air. Closing her eyes, she felt a tingling sensation in her toes that began to rise and build as it worked its way up through her fairy body. She could hear the tiger growling but tried not to let it break her concentration. She held out her arms as the tingling rippled down the length of them to become a throbbing in her fingertips. And then a light breeze brushed her face and rustled her hair. Opening her eyes, she saw the long grass around them undulating like waves, as if a ball of wind were gently orbiting around them. The tiger turned its head, curious as to what was happening. Then smoke started to rise from the tips of the grass, and the smoke became a flame. A circle of fire was growing around the tiger, and as Rowan's friends looked on in astonishment, the animal began to cower away, its ears flattened back against its head.

"Did Rowan just set the grass on fire?" Willow whispered to Harold.

Harold looked as amazed as the rest of them. "Yes, I believe she did."

"Take that, Tigger!" yelled Aiken.

Rowan ignored Aiken, keeping her focus firmly on

the tiger. "No, I don't want you to be afraid of me." Holding her arms aloft again, with her eyes tight shut, she began to feel droplets of water speckle her arms. She raised her face to the sky, and a warm rain fell onto it. Her mother had always turned her face to meet the rain, and Rowan smiled with the memory of it. She felt like her mother was looking out for her even when she wasn't there. When Rowan opened her eyes again, she could see the grass steaming where the rain had put out the flames. The tiger had laid itself down on the grass, and its head was resting on a paw. Rowan drifted slowly toward it and reached out a hand to stroke its forehead. The fur felt strong but incredibly soft. The tiger made a contented purring sound.

"Be my friend," said Rowan, gently settling herself down onto the animal's head and speaking in soft, hushed tones.

The tiger rose slowly to its feet in response as the others looked back at her in awe.

"It's as easy as that, then," murmured Olor.

"Bit different from riding a robin," said Aiken to Harold under his breath.

They followed Rowan and the tiger as it led the way

majestically out of the enclosure. When they arrived back out in the zoo, Jack was waiting, seated astride a dark, mottled canine creature with disproportionately large-looking ears. Jack looked at Rowan and the tiger, openmouthed.

"Like your pooch," said Aiken as he and the squirrel monkey sauntered past Jack.

"It's an African hunting dog," said Jack, rather annoyed.

"I think I'd like to find a friend now too," said Olor.

"I want a pony!" said Willow brightly.

"Okay," said Harold. "It's a big zoo, and we don't have much time."

Rowan whispered into the tiger's ear, "Let's go . . . Tigris."

* Chapter Eight *
ROWAN'S ARK

It was one of the strangest rescue teams ever assembled, but it was now complete. Rowan rode on the back of the tiger, Jack held on to the neck of his hunting dog, Aiken was clinging to his squirrel monkey as it swung through the branches above, Olor was sitting astride a sleek-looking otter, and Willow looked as proud as Punch on the head of a small zebra. Harold was flying above, looking for the canal.

"This way!" he shouted to the crew.

When they arrived at the canal, they saw an empty narrowboat tied up on the other side of the water. It was the kind of boat that got used for pleasure cruises and was open at the front. After spying a bridge a little farther along, they steered their steeds over the canal and back down the towpath to the boat.

"Okay, how do we untie it?" asked Rowan.

"Fingers isn't strong enough to undo the knot," said Aiken.

"One of the beasts will have to gnaw through it, then," said Harold.

Rowan leaned into Tigris's ear to offer instructions, and the big cat's formidable bite snapped clean through the rope.

"I think I'd have waited until we were *on* the boat," said Harold, as the narrowboat started drifting away, with the end of the rope dangling in the water.

"I'll get it!" shouted Olor, urging her otter into the canal. The animal slunk into the dark water, and its sleek body shimmied effortlessly toward the rope. After gripping the frayed end with its sharp teeth, the otter began to pull the boat back to the bank. But the rope wasn't long enough and pulled taut short of the canal bank. Worse, the boat was beginning to pull the otter backward and out into the middle of the canal.

"Come on, Tigris," said Rowan.

She spurred the tiger on, and it took an almighty leap into the water, soaking them all in a huge splash. Tigris swam after the rope that was trailing from the departing boat, and after grabbing it in her powerful jaws, she returned the boat to the shore. The tiger heaved herself out of the canal and held the rope while the motley crew trooped onto the vessel. Once they were all safely on the boat, Tigris jumped in herself and shook herself dry like a dog that had been swimming in a lake, soaking everyone on board in the process.

"Now, how do we drive this thing?" asked Willow, wiping bits of pondweed out of her hair. The narrow boat began drifting around in a circle.

"There must be a key to start an engine somewhere . . . ," said Rowan.

"Like this?" said Aiken, hauling an ignition key as big as himself from beneath a plant pot, where it had been hidden.

"To put in here?" said Olor, opening a small cupboard door to reveal a keyhole and a series of lights.

Rowan smiled. She'd missed her fairy team.

"Okay, Aiken," Rowan said. "Can Fingers turn the key in the ignition?"

Fingers seemed to know what Rowan was asking and grabbed the key from Aiken almost before she'd finished speaking. He scampered over to the cupboard and started slapping the key against the lights.

"In the hole, Fingers!" shouted Aiken.

Fingers responded by attempting to insert the key the wrong way around.

"He's not the smartest animal in the zoo, is he?" said Jack to Harold a little dismissively.

"He's trying his best," said Willow as Fingers finally pushed the key into the ignition the right way around and gave it a turn from the off position to the start position. But nothing happened. The boat was starting to turn and drift again now, edging dangerously near to another boat tied up against the bank. Rowan buzzed to the boat's tiller to try to stop the narrow boat from hitting the other boat.

"Help!" she cried to Aiken and Olor, but they weren't strong enough to halt the motion.

"Don't worry!" cried Willow, who then whispered into her zebra's ear. The striped animal clattered over to the back of the boat and nuzzled the tiller with its head until the tiller straightened up. The narrowboat glided past the other vessel, missing it by centimeters. "Keep trying the key, Fingers!" Willow called.

This time it caught and the engine spluttered into life, making a noise more like you'd expect from a tractor, not a boat.

"We're sailing!" shouted Rowan to Willow above the engine noise. They exchanged a look, and Rowan nodded to her sister as if to say, *Well done.*

"Aye, aye, Captain Sister!" said Willow, lifting her hand to her brow in salute.

Rowan looked back down the boat at its strange assembly of wet and slightly shivering occupants. The zebra at the tiller with its back half inside the wheelhouse, and its head and neck sticking out to steer; Olor sitting next to Willow between its ears, issuing instructions while the otter chased Fingers and Aiken around the boat; at the front, the tiger was stretched out along a bench on one side, her eyes firmly fixed on the hunting dog pacing along a bench on the other side with Jack riding on its back and trying to keep it under control. The tiger and the dog clearly didn't like being in such close quarters.

"Just like Rowan's Ark," said Harold, landing next to her.

"Hmmm," said Rowan. "Only, Noah built the ark to get away from trouble. We've got one to take us toward it."

"It is what it is," replied Harold mischievously.

Rowan looked at him sideways. "We need to have a rule about that."

Harold's eyes twinkled. "So what's your plan, Rowan?" he asked.

Rowan stared down into the black water sloshing past the boat, wishing that she had one.

The reflection of the moon shimmered in the dark canal as Willow steered the long boat out of Regent's Park and through Primrose Hill. There was no one around at first, but as they neared Camden, they heard shouts and laughter around the bend. Worried they might be discovered, Rowan thought quickly, seeing that there were rolled-up canvas blinds tied all the way around the front of the boat.

"Aiken! The blinds!"

Aiken understood and made Fingers scamper up to untie the cords so that the blinds fell to cover the windows. In no time at all the fairies and their beasts were hidden from view. Just in time too, as they passed under a bridge and turned a corner to see the way ahead blocked by huge wooden gates in the water. And off to either side there were throngs of people milling around in the bars and restaurants above. Rowan asked Fingers to turn the engine off, and they glided to a halt in a narrow channel just before the gates. The zebra ducked its head inside the wheelhouse, and from the outside it looked like a normal narrowboat. On the inside, however, it was very different.

"What *is* this place?" whispered Rowan to Harold urgently.

"It's Camden Lock," he replied. "In the middle of Camden Market."

"What in the Realms are we going to—"

"What's a lock?" interrupted Willow.

Rowan sighed. She had more pressing things to worry about than explaining how canals worked.

"It raises or lowers boats between different levels of water on a canal," said Harold.

"Like the elevator in our apartment building?"

"If you like."

"Please, Willow," said Rowan. "I'm trying to think,

and it would be really helpful if you'd be quiet for just a minute."

"Right, well I hope this one works better than our elevator does," said Willow, ignoring her sister and whispering into her zebra's ear.

The zebra clattered forward with Willow perched on its head, squeezed out into the open, and took a great leap off the boat and onto the bank.

"What? No!" Rowan buzzed after Willow to try to stop her, but shrank back under cover when she saw all the people. *"Will-owww!"* she half-shouted, half-growled.

From her hiding place Rowan could see the people a little more clearly now. It was obviously not a normal night out. There were fire-breathers, jugglers, people dressed in all manner of exotic clothes, and hair dyed more colors than Rowan had even known existed. And, for the moment at least, they seemed not to be noticing the zebra standing on the bank trying to nudge the lock gates open with its head. In fact, the zebra was one of the less strange sights to be seen.

For an instant it seemed like what Willow was doing might just work, until Rowan turned her head to see a young woman sitting on the lock gate on the side opposite Willow and the zebra. She had fluorescent yellow hair twirled into two small buns on either side of her head. It looked like she'd been crying. Now, however, she was just wide-eyed with amazement, staring at Willow and her stripy friend.

"Hide, Willow!" hissed Rowan, hoping that the woman wouldn't hear. Willow ignored Rowan yet again.

"EXCUSE ME!" yelled Willow. "WE NEED SOME HELP WITH THE ELEVATOR!"

The woman couldn't hear her, so Willow took some very awkward flying hops across the gate to perch in front of her. Rowan winced as Willow very nearly fell into the canal.

"Haven't quite got the hang of the flying thing yet," explained Willow to the woman.

The woman just nodded and rubbed the tears from her eyes, struck dumb by the sight of what could only be a fairy telling a zebra to open one of the gates at Camden Lock.

"Are you okay?" asked Willow. "You look like you're upset."

"Can I just ask if this is real?" asked the woman. "It's been a long night."

"Oh yes," Willow said, beaming as Fingers scampered through the woman's legs, chased by the otter.

The woman banged the side of her head with the palm of her hand as if to knock herself sensible. "Okay, if this is a dream, I'm just going to go with it," she said as much to herself as to Willow.

Willow patted the woman's leg to reassure her. "My sister says it's fine to cry, by the way. She says it's 'an important part of the process.'"

"She's—she's very wise, your sister," the woman stuttered.

Willow nodded. "I know. She's just in that boat there with our other fairy friends and a tiger we just broke out of the zoo. We're going to rescue our mom and save the Fairy Realms from destruction."

The woman looked even more bewildered.

"Would you mind pushing this other gate open so we can get through?" asked Willow brightly. "We need some help getting up in this elevator."

"Okaaaay," said the woman, looking around to see if anyone else was seeing what she was seeing. "I guess we can't have those fairy things being destroyed."

"Fairy Realms," confirmed Willow.

"Yep, those," said the woman, standing up a little shakily to push the gate.

Between the woman and the zebra, the lock gates were opened, and water began pouring through, slowly raising the boat upward, as if by magic.

Willow beamed with pride. "Thanks for your help!"

The zebra stepped gingerly back onto the boat, followed by the squirrel monkey and the otter.

"My pleasure," said the woman. "Good luck rescuing . . . your mom."

Fingers turned the ignition key again, and the boat powered forward.

Willow waved to the woman as they slid past her along the canal. The still-dazed woman waved back.

"See," Willow said to Rowan. "This is going to be a breeze."

Rowan sighed but couldn't stop a small smile from creeping onto her face. She turned away so Willow couldn't see that she was just a tiny bit proud of her sister. This time, at least. There was still a long way to go.

"You need a name for your zebra," said Rowan as they motored down the canal.

Willow thought for a second.

"What are you calling your otter, Olor?"

"I saw her name on the sign in the zoo. I think it's in Latin," replied Olor. "She's called Lutra."

"Nice," said Willow. "I think I'll call my zebra . . . Spot."

Rowan rolled her eyes.

"Perfect!" laughed Aiken.

* Chapter Nine *
A TIGER BY THE TAIL

They forged ahead through the night, safe in the knowledge that no one knew their little narrowboat's amazing secret. The boat cut through the water at some speed, navigating locks expertly now that Spot and Willow knew what they were doing, even passing undaunted through a long foreboding tunnel—despite Aiken's getting a bit scared of the dark. Finally they made it out into a basin filled with all manner of craft, and from the smell and the sound, they could tell they were close to the great River Thames. One last lock and they were through and out onto the open water.

"This is the life!" said Willow.

"Arrrgh!" Aiken did his best pirate impression, pretending he had a wooden leg. "Life on the open waves."

The wind and the movement of the river buffeted the boat more strongly than the still water of the canal, but Rowan allowed herself to relax a little. They were getting closer to Mom. If there was any kind of plan, it was working.

"What's that?" asked Olor, pointing out through the parted blinds to the dark river ahead.

Rowan's heart sank immediately. It wasn't going to be good, was it? Couldn't she have a moment of calm? Just a little time when she didn't have to worry?

"Oh, that's nothing," said Willow, doing a fluttery jump from the top of Spot's head to see what was coming toward them. "Just a party boat."

"A party boat?" Rowan flew up to join Willow on top of Spot's head. Her eyes grew wide with fear. It was a large pleasure cruiser, blaring music, filled with people, and it was steaming straight for them.

"It can't see us!" said Rowan. "We're not supposed to be on the river; we don't have any lights. Turn to port!"

"Turn to what?" asked Willow.

"TO THE LEFT!" shouted Rowan.

Willow spoke into Spot's ear, and he pushed hard

against the tiller, turning their little craft toward the riverbank. The pleasure boat was still bearing down on them, not changing course. At the last minute the captain of the other boat must have seen them, as a horn blared out, deafening the lot of them. The dog started barking, and the tiger growled in response. The pleasure boat missed them by a whisker but still sent them rolling in its wake. Spot stumbled and fell; the dog slid off its bench and smacked straight into Tigris, making her roar. Lutra and Fingers scrabbled for something to hold on to. With no one manning the tiller, it swung free, and the boat began to drift helplessly toward the riverbank. Rowan could see what was happening but was powerless to do anything about it. Before they knew it, they heard an almighty grating sound, and then they felt the unmistakable shuddering of running aground.

Willow was the one to break the stunned silence. "Are we going to get into trouble for crashing the boat?"

"Ow, my head," said Aiken, rubbing it with his hand.

Rowan poked her head out of the blinds to see the

extent of the damage. The narrowboat was stranded at a forty-five-degree angle next to a scraggly bit of rocky beach by the side of the Thames. The boat was still half in the river, but the water was probably only about a meter deep where they were stuck. There was no way they were going to get the vessel afloat again. Just across the beach there was a set of stone steps that led up to the road above. As Rowan strained her eyes to see as far as she could, two pinpricks of light and a flash of orange whipped across her field of vision.

"Fox!" yelled Aiken.

The hunting dog went wild. It raced around the small boat, desperate to get onto the shore and after the fox. Jack had been lying on its back and was now hanging on to the scruff of its neck, frantically trying to slow it down. The dog barreled into Willow, knocking her sideways, then crashed into the tiger, who rose to her feet and snarled. The dog suddenly leapt through the blinds, clearing the water, and skittered onto the shore, Jack still swinging from side to side on its back. It hared up the steps after the fox, and Jack and the dog disappeared into the night.

"Follow that dog!" shouted Rowan.

The fairies each mounted their beasts and encouraged them to leap from the boat, and the crew all splashed through the water to the shore. Up the steps, they all stood on the edge of a little square surrounded by blocks of apartments. There were at least four different directions that Jack and the dog could have gone in. But before Rowan had to make a decision, Tigris started to growl. Her tail twitched, and she sprang forward across the square.

"She must be able to smell the dog," said Rowan. "Follow us!"

Rowan prayed that Jack wouldn't be far. It may have been nighttime, but they were still guiding a tiger, a zebra, a monkey, and an otter through the streets of London. They had no choice but to be out in the open. At least this part of town was pretty quiet at night. There were a few lights in the windows of the apartments but no one wandering around. Yet.

"This is AMAZING!" yelled Willow at the top of her voice as they galloped out onto a road, lit from above by orangey fluorescent streetlights. Olor and Lutra and Aiken and Fingers were all clinging on to Spot's back as Willow rode atop his head. Harold flew above them, and Rowan held on to Tigris's ears. Rowan couldn't enjoy it like Willow was. She was too worried about what was coming next. And what if something happened to Willow? It would be all her fault—

"Look!" shouted Olor, breaking Rowan's concentration.

"Is it Jack?" yelled Rowan.

Olor just pointed ahead. Rowan followed her finger to an enormous warehouse-like building lit up like a football stadium at night. Where everything around it was quiet, this was a hive of activity. Large white vans were parked all about, and people dressed all in white were trooping in and out carrying large white polystyrene boxes. The cogs whirred around in Rowan's head. Tigris hadn't been chasing after the dog; she'd caught the scent of something else entirely. They were racing toward Billingsgate Market, one of the largest markets in the country for fresh fish.

Rowan shouted into Tigris's ear to try to stop her, but the tiger seemed hypnotized by the smell of the fish. Tigris was surely ravenous after the night's exertions. Rowan took one look at all the rapidly approaching people, and one look back at her sister and friends.

She couldn't risk them being hurt or captured.

"Stay here!" she yelled to the others. "I can't stop Tigris. I'll find you again, I promise!"

"We can help!" shouted Willow.

"NO!" replied Rowan firmly. "I need to know you're safe."

"But—"

Willow wasn't giving up, and Rowan knew there was only one thing to stop her. "You'll get in the way, Willow. THIS IS UP TO ME." And before Aiken and Olor could open their mouths to protest, she continued, "And I need you two to look after her!"

Rowan could see Willow sadly leaning into Spot's ear and slowing the zebra down. The tiger accelerated away, with Harold flying alongside, and Rowan had no time to regret her words. As they dashed toward the entrance, Rowan could see the white-coated men in front of them diving out of the way left and right, wide-eyed with fear. Some threw the boxes they were carrying into the air, sending fish and the ice cubes they were packed in flying; others used the boxes to try to repel the striped invader.

For Tigris, it seemed to be a complete sensory

overload. She clearly didn't know which way to turn. She careered right into the middle of the market, bounding this way and that, scattering deliverymen and market workers as she went. Rowan was doing all she could just to hold on. Finally Tigris clamped her jaws on to a large salmon that one of the men had thrown in front of her. Rowan was able to look around her at last, but wasn't happy about what she saw. The white-coated men were starting to emerge from their hiding places now that the tiger was engaged with its evening meal. As Harold twittered helplessly above, the men were slowly revealing long knives for gutting fish, the shiny steel glinting in the harsh overhead lights. As best she could Rowan crawled into Tigris's ear to hide, but the men were far too concerned about the tiger in their fish market to even notice the fairy on its head. Rowan shrank away in fear of the men creeping nearer and nearer. There was no way out of this.

Just then a clatter of hooves and a flash of stripes made everyone turn around. Jaws hit the floor in shock, and a few knives followed. Surely there wasn't a tiger *and* a zebra in the middle of Billingsgate Market?

"Get your phone out, Asif," whispered one stallholder to his teenage son. The lad held up his phone as if to video what was happening. "To call the zoo, idiot boy!"

But there was no time for that either, as off the back of the zebra jumped a squirrel monkey and an otter, darting off in different directions. Lutra grabbed a small fish between her teeth and ran through everyone's legs, scattering them this way and that. Fingers swung along the yellow metal gantry above their heads like a miniature Tarzan. Harold fluttered from side to side, causing as much of a nuisance as he could. Hidden in Spot's mane, Willow, Aiken, and Olor orchestrated the operation. Spot bolted toward Tigris, forcing the men with knives to duck out of the way.

"Let's go, Sis!" shouted Willow as they passed Tigris.

"I thought I told you to wait outside!" replied Rowan, although she was very glad for once that Willow hadn't listened.

The fish fell from Tigris's jaws, and Rowan just had time to grip two handfuls of fur before the tiger sprang into action. They chased after the zebra, crashing through crates and sending the fishmongers diving for cover again. Tigris's claws scraped against the wet concrete floor, struggling to get a purchase as she drove toward the great door on the other side of the market. But the closer they got, the smaller the door seemed to be getting. A white coat had hit the button to lower the enormous electric door, and the barrier was slowly but surely grinding downward. Tigris responded by running even faster. They were going to either make it by a whisker or smash headlong into the metal. Ahead of them, Spot and his fairy passengers careered through the opening. Lutra and Fingers followed quickly after.

Rowan gritted her teeth and held on more tightly. They were going to make it. They would have to make it. The gap between the bottom of the door and the floor looked too narrow, and she couldn't bear to look. Tigris leapt and skidded flat across the concrete, and sailed clean through and into the fresh air beyond. They spun to look behind them as the metal door was about to clunk closed, but at the very last minute Harold swooped out through the thin sliver of light before the barricade snapped shut.

"Take *that*!" yelled Aiken, punching the air. "What a ride!"

Sirens started blaring in the distance.

"We have to keep moving," said Rowan.

"Can't we just, you know"—Aiken pointed back at the door they'd just made it through—"enjoy that for a bit?"

Olor clouted him on the head.

"What? What did I say?" asked Aiken.

"What about Jack?" asked Willow. "And the dog?"

"There's nothing we can do right now," said Rowan. "If they were chasing after a fox, there's a good chance it will have taken them straight back to its master at Greenwich Park. No one's going to notice an African hunting dog out on the streets in the same way they'd notice a tiger and a zebra. I think they'll be okay."

"We have a bigger problem than that," said Harold, looking toward the shore. Everyone turned to face him. "I think we're stuck on the wrong side of the river without a boat."

Chapter Ten

ACROSS THE RIVER

Sylvia could feel her daughters getting closer. She looked out at the twinkling city and knew that Rowan wouldn't stop until she made it. Rowan's determination made Sylvia proud, but it also made her fearful. She looked down from her treetop prison and saw foxes and fairies swarming below. Rowan would be met by a whole army of them. Even her resourceful daughter would surely be overwhelmed. Sylvia strained against the bonds that held her arms and wings. She began to rub them against the rough bark of the tree in the hope that she could free herself and stop Rowan from needing to do it for her.

"We've just had word," said the bitter-chocolate voice, stopping her in her tracks. "She's been sighted—would you believe—riding a *tiger*."

Sylvia turned to face Vulpes, trying to hide behind her the evidence that she'd been attempting to escape. She was unsure whether or not to believe him, but it was surely far too crazy a thing for him just to make up.

"Somewhat beggars belief, doesn't it?" he continued, pacing around her. "What *will* she think of next? Is she going to arrive on a giraffe? With an army of aardvarks?"

"You're worried, aren't you?" said Sylvia.

Vulpes narrowed his eyes.

"A lot less concerned than *you* are," he replied, clapping his hands and summoning a fairy rider. "Bring the girl to me alive," he said to the rider. "Do with the others what you will." Then Vulpes made as if to launch off the tree into the air, but a thought stopped him. "Including the other daughter. I have no need for her."

Vulpes leapt into the darkness and away. Sylvia looked up at the stars, hoping that one would fall so that she could make a wish. But it didn't. So she kept on scraping her ties on the tree, because it was all she could do.

Rowan, Aiken, Olor, and Harold were all riding on Tigris's back now, and the tiger was stalking as stealthily as it could through the shadows, avoiding the harsh lights from the streetlamps. Willow and the zebra trotted alongside with Lutra and Fingers at their heels. Off in the distance sirens wailed, but the fairies focused grimly on the matter at hand.

"What do we do now?" asked Aiken.

Everyone looked at Rowan, because that's what they did in these situations. Rowan shuffled uncomfortably in her seat. She had no idea what they should do now, but she felt like she needed to say something.

"Let's head for the river," she said.

The group pulled off the road and along a tree-lined path that led around a small marina, and looked to see where the boats must have come in off the Thames. A couple of minutes later they were back by the powerful river's edge. Only, this time there were no boats on hand to steal. Only a quarter of a mile of cold, black water between them and the road to Greenwich. Across the river, lit up like a gigantic beacon mocking their inability to reach it, stood the tented stadium of the O2 arena.

"How in the Realms . . . ?" said Aiken.

"There's no way across," agreed Olor.

They all slumped a little, staring out into the darkness with the breeze ruffling their wings.

"Can't we fly over it?" asked Willow.

Olor held up her wings, and white feathers seesawed to the ground.

"It hurts just to hold these in the air," said Olor. "Never mind fly across a river."

"No, Willow's right," said Rowan. "We can."

All the heads spun back to Rowan.

"How's Harold going to carry a tiger on his back?" said Aiken dismissively.

"He's not," said Rowan. "We'll all fly on the Air Line."

"We're going to the airport?" asked a mystified Aiken.

"No, the *Air Line*." Rowan pointed into the distance, to the left of the O2, where huge pillars were rising from the water in a line across the river. "The cable car."

Before long the group had picked their way along the shoreline around the bend in the river and arrived at the large glass-walled cable car station on the Royal Docks. There was only one problem.

"It's shut?" said Olor.

Fingers hung off a door handle and shook it as if to confirm, without a doubt, that the cable station was locked. But Rowan wasn't going to be deterred that easily. She looked the building up and down, searching for the solution. It was two stories high, the ground floor all glass doors and windows, but the front of the upper floor was open where the cable cars came and went.

"The hole in the front," said Rowan. "Let's go."

Harold and the fairies set off skyward, their wings sounding triumphant chords as they did so.

"Is anyone ever going to teach me to fly?" asked Willow, flapping around back on the ground below them, like a bird with an injured wing. Rowan had forgotten that Willow wasn't yet able to fly like them.

"We need you to look after the beasts, Willow," Rowan shouted down to her, trying to make Willow think it was all part of her plan. "We'll let you in in a second. Keep them out of sight until we do."

Willow put on a brave face, but Rowan could tell she hated being left out. Willow ushered the tiger and the zebra around the back of the building away from the road. The otter slipped into the river, happy to have some time back in the water. Rowan, Harold, and the other fairies flew up to the opening and swooped into the top of the building, while Fingers nimbly scrambled up after them.

"Spread out," said Rowan. "We need to find the keys to open the door, and a way to start the cable car running."

"Nothing major, then," mumbled Aiken under his breath.

"We heard that, Oakwing," teased Olor.

The group scoured the building from top to bottom. But to no avail. Rowan arrived back down on the ground floor, but on the other side of the glass entrance door from where Willow was waiting for news.

"WE CAN'T FIND THE KEYS!" Rowan shouted.

Willow pointed to her ears to show that she couldn't hear, getting as close to the glass as she could.

Rowan made a big shrugging gesture to try to explain a different way. But then she noticed something behind Willow. Something far more disturbing. She banged on the glass to warn her sister.

"BEHIND YOU!" she yelled. "FOX!"

Willow pointed at her ears again. Rowan could see that she was mouthing "Can't hear you."

Rowan banged harder on the glass and jabbed her finger to point behind Willow.

"RUN!" she hollered at her little sister.

Willow turned to see what Rowan was pointing at. A sleek, muscular, rust-colored fox was creeping toward her. Willow started to flap her wings, desperately trying to take off, but she could get only about a meter into the air before falling back to the ground.

"Help! Tigris! Spot!" shouted Willow, but the beasts were too far away to hear her.

"Help! Harold!" shouted Rowan from the other side of the glass, but she couldn't locate any of her friends in the building.

Rowan made a superfast mental calculation. Could she get back upstairs, out of the building, and down to Willow before the fox struck? No. It was never going to happen. She was paralyzed, trapped behind the glass and forced to watch, like a boxer's punching bag being pummeled by her worst fears. She banged on the glass again and again, as if that might scare the fox away. But the fox was going to get her sister; there was nothing she could do. Even her powers wouldn't help, stuck behind the glass. And it was all her fault. All. Rowan's. Fault.

She watched helplessly as the fox pounced toward Willow, with its jaws wide, its claws extended. But then something she didn't expect happened. At the very moment when the fox was about to land on top of her, Willow made her own almighty leap, beating her wings furiously as if her life depended on it. Because it did. And instead of slamming back to the ground, this time Willow rose gracefully into the air to wheel high above the fox like an eagle riding a thermal.

"I'M DOING IT!" yelled Willow.

"You're doing it," whispered Rowan to herself.

The fox landed in a heap and twisted around to see where its prey had disappeared to. But instead of looking up to see Willow, it found itself staring into the face of a tiger.

ROARRRR! Tigris had her ears pinned back and all her teeth bared. It was a terrifying sight.

Rowan had never seen a fox move so fast in her life. Its claws scrabbled at the concrete, propelling it out from under the tiger and off into the darkness. Willow landed with a gentle *plonk* on Tigris's head.

"Thanks, kitty," Willow said, blowing Tigris a little kiss. "Better late than never."

Rowan felt her shoulders drop with a sense of enormous relief. She could almost cry.

"Hiya!" It was Aiken. "We found these on a sleeping security guard." Fingers was next to him wearing a metal ring full of keys like a necklace. "Did we miss anything?"

"What? Oh, no," said Rowan, who couldn't even begin to explain. "Pretty uneventful here."

"Good, good," said Aiken. "Shall we get a move on, then?"

Rowan and Aiken heaved the keys up to a lock in the door and tried each of them until finally one clicked. On the other side of the glass, where Spot and a dripping wet Lutra had now joined her, Willow corralled the animals into pushing open the door. At last they were all reunited. Rowan pulled her sister into an almighty hug. The kind of hug you never want to end.

"Steady on," said Aiken. "You only just saw her five minutes ago."

"Don't scare me like that again," Rowan said, ignoring Aiken.

"Safe as houses, Sis," said Willow. "You don't have to worry about Willow Pillow."

Rowan smiled. But she wasn't quite convinced.

"So, how do we get this thing started?" asked Olor.

"I don't suppose it would be as simple as that, would it?" said Harold, pointing his wing up at what looked like a huge red buzzer on the wall.

"Only one way to find out," said Aiken, riding Fingers over to investigate.

"Unless it's the alarm?" said Olor.

Fingers took one look and full-on head-butted the button. Almost immediately the machinery began to whir and clank, and a cable car started to swing along its rail toward them. As it drew nearer, the doors pulled back to reveal two benches on either side, big enough for three humans to sit on each.

"Everyone in!" said Rowan. "We don't know how long we've got till the guard wakes up."

Tigris padded in first, then circled and jumped up onto one of the benches, before waiting like a sphinx for the others. The car was still moving, so they had to be quick. Spot was next, clattering into the space between the benches. Lutra and Fingers took up residence on the opposite bench, and just as the doors began to close, Harold and the fairies all buzzed in to join them. It was a tight squeeze, but they'd made it. The car whooshed up and out of the building, dangling along the wire that would carry them across the river.

"It's so beautiful!" said Willow, pointing out the window.

And indeed it was. The skyscrapers in the city of London were lit up like a forest of Christmas trees as the group flew effortlessly over the mighty black river that had seemed so impassable only moments before.

"We're coming, Mom," whispered Rowan under her breath.

"We're coming." Willow put a hand on her sister's shoulder and smiled.

Rowan smiled back, but she knew that the hardest part was yet to come. She looked around the cable car at the motley band of fairies and beasts crammed into the small space. She hoped that reinforcements were on their way from the other parks, because there was no way that this lot could take on an army of foxes by itself.

The cable car clunked down into the station on the other side of the river.

"Everyone out!" yelled Harold as the doors opened. "Fingers, the keys!"

Back on the first side of the river, a security guard woke up with a start, patting his trouser pockets for something, before realizing that what had woken him up was in fact the sound of the cable car in operation. He jumped to his feet, knocking to the floor the embroidery he'd been doing, and rushed down to shut off the machine. He scratched his head, wondering just how it had started all by itself.

The fairies were now astride their beasts once again, keeping as far away from any sign of life as they could. They sneaked along, trying to draw as little attention to themselves as possible. Hugging the shoreline, they circled around the giant O2 arena. Before long an imposing old white building rose up on their left that looked a bit as though Buckingham Palace and two mini St. Paul's Cathedrals had been squashed together.

"This is where we turn left," said Harold. "Old Royal Naval College. On the other side is the park, and your mother."

They slipped up a side road past the naval college until a great, black wrought iron gate blocked their path to the dark green depths of Greenwich Park beyond. Well, it barred the way of the tiger and the zebra, at least. Rowan slumped in defeat.

"Next time," said Aiken, "you might want to pick a smaller beast. . . ."

Chapter Eleven

BETRAYAL

There were huge padlocks on the gate, and no sleeping security guards to steal keys from. And the railings themselves must have been three meters high. Olor and Aiken guided Lutra and Fingers through the bars, but Tigris and Spot were another matter. There was no way they could jump over the railings. The fairies might be able to get into the park, but the beasts they needed to fight the foxes would be stuck outside.

Rowan searched around for something, anything that might help their cause. Just to the side of the gate was a litter bin, and behind that a pillar the same height as the gate.

Rowan gave instructions to Tigris.

Although there was precious little room on top of the bin for a tiger, Tigris managed to scramble on top of it, and from there to the top of the pillar. Rowan breathed a small sigh of relief. But Tigris still had to get down.

While Willow stayed with Spot, Rowan and Harold slipped through the railings to await Tigris on the other side. A single streetlamp lit their expectant faces from above.

"Come on, Tigris! You can do it!" shouted Aiken.

She was three meters up, peering down at the spiked ends of the gate railings on one side and the top of the hedge on the other. This time a front paw slipped over the edge, and she lurched forward before catching herself. Rowan put her hand to her mouth.

At that moment a howl rang out in the darkness, but not from any of them. It was joined by a chorus of others, like a rallying cry. The fairies turned to try to see where the noise was coming from, but it was coming from all around them. All of a sudden they could see dozens of eyes blinking in the dark, bobbing forward into the light. Foxes. A whole unruly mob of them was upon the fairies in an instant. Lutra and Fingers scattered, and the fairies scrambled into the air to dodge the orange-furred jaws of their attackers.

Tigris tried to leap forward, but in her haste to get at the foxes, she slipped slightly, caught a paw on the spiked gate, and landed awkwardly on the ground, roaring with pain. The foxes saw their chance, and a team of five of them set upon the stricken tiger.

"No!" screamed Willow, dashing over to help.

"Stay there!" yelled Rowan, trying to keep Willow safely on the other side of the iron bars.

Tigris rolled from side to side, trying to throw the foxes off, but they were like dogs with a bone, refusing to let go. Harold and the fairies rushed to her aid but were swatted away like flies. Rowan thought quickly. Soaring into the air, she cleared her mind and began to spin. She tried to put all apprehension to the back of her mind. What if it didn't work again? She refused to be distracted by what was going on around her. Soon she felt that familiar strength pound through her muscles, stretching and twisting as it did so. She fell back to the earth as an African hunting dog. Quick, aggressive, and angry. Willow's mouth dropped open in shock and awe.

Rowan the dog clamped her razor-sharp jaws around the tail of one of the foxes, biting down hard until the fox yelped in pain and was forced to let go of the tiger. Rowan flung the fox by the tail, sending it scurrying away into the darkness, then repeated the action with the next assailant. Before long Tigris was able to regain her feet, letting out an almighty roar that scared off the remaining foxes. With her attackers gone, Tigris collapsed back to the ground, breathing hard and nursing her injured paw. Rowan returned to fairy form, equally exhausted.

"Cool trick, Rowan," said Willow.

"This was just a warning," said Harold when the dazed friends had come back to their senses. "There's a whole army of them waiting for us in there." He pointed his beak into the middle of the park.

"Oh, Harold," said Aiken. "You always know just the right thing to say to make us feel better."

Rowan and Olor shared a rueful smile, which quickly melted away as Rowan realized Spot was still stuck outside the park.

"Rowan." Aiken turned to Rowan expectantly. "Can't you just magic Spot over the fence?"

Rowan felt the weight of responsibility and expectation fall upon her again.

"That's not how it works, Aiken," Harold cut in. "Rowan has the power of transformation, not levitation."

"What about all the rain and wind stuff she can do?" asked Aiken.

"Have you ever seen the rain pick a lock, or the wind lift a zebra three meters into the air?" replied Harold. "She has some sort of power over nature and the elements, but we need more than weather right now."

That seemed to satisfy Aiken, but it was of no help to Rowan. She already knew there was no way they were going to get the zebra over that gate.

"Is there any other way into the park, Harold?" Rowan asked, trying to be practical.

"I don't know," replied Harold.

Then another realization kicked in.

"So if the GodMother convinces Cervus to bring the deer to fight with us, they might be stuck outside too?" said Rowan.

"Perhaps," he said.

Rowan felt deflated. She looked to the sky. "It's nearly dawn," Rowan said. "The GodMother will be here soon to meet us. And then we'll know."

"There's no time to wait for the GodMother," came a voice from the shadows.

They all spun around to see Jack astride his hunting dog, swaggering toward them like a cowboy on the back of his favorite horse.

"Where have *you* been all this time?" said Olor, clearly unimpressed. "We could have done with some help."

"I've been waiting for you slow coaches," replied Jack. "And finding out some very useful information."

"Like what?" asked Aiken.

"Like Vulpes is about to destroy the weeping beech of Greenwich Park," said Jack.

"What makes you so sure, Jack?" asked Rowan.

"Don't you trust me?" asked Jack in return. "I could hear them plotting. In their lair beneath a tree."

Rowan stared at Jack and narrowed her eyes, as if she were trying to see through him. Jack seemed to squirm a little in his seat. Rowan knew Jack wasn't the most reliable fairy, but why would he lie?

"Your mother needs you," said Jack.

They were only four small words, but they were like an electric shock to Rowan, stinging her into action. "We need to go," she said. "Now."

Harold looked troubled. "Given our lack of resources, I think it would be prudent to wait for the GodMother."

Rowan snapped. "Prudent to wait? We don't have time for that, Harold! What about the tree? What about our mom?" Rowan turned to her sister. "Willow, you're safer on the other side of those bars."

"Again?" said Willow. "No, I'm coming this time, Rowan. I can look after myself." And with that she patted Spot on the neck and arrowed through the railings to land next to Rowan on Tigris's head.

Rowan raised her eyes heavenward. It was never easy, was it?

"All right," said Rowan. "Lead on, Jack."

Jack wheeled his dog around and took off in the direction toward which the foxes had retreated. Willow waved good-bye to the zebra, who whinnied a reply, and the group set off after Jack, with Harold trailing reluctantly behind.

The gang ventured deep into Greenwich Park—the Realm of the Fairies of the Fox—right into the very heart of their enemy's territory. Olor sat astride her scampering otter, Aiken clung on to his erratic monkey, and Rowan and Willow shared a space upon the tiger's head as she limped forward, her injured paw still causing her pain. Jack rode ahead on the nervy hunting dog, or rather held it back, as it constantly seemed to want to tear off somewhere, and Harold flew zigzags from tree to tree behind them.

The part of the park they had entered was low, flat, and wide, with the occasional dark tree breaking up the expanse of grassy green. They strode along a tree-lined path that cut through the middle, but in front of them the ground rose up—a wooded hill to their left and another hill in the distance to their right topped by two buildings.

"The Royal Observatory," explained Harold as Rowan puzzled over what the strange globe-shaped building might be.

"Very interesting," said Aiken, clearly not meaning it. "But is that where Vulpes lives?"

"Nearby," replied Jack, overhearing.

They could faintly see some movement on the ground to the left of the observatory.

"Just there," said Jack. "In those trees."

"It looks very quiet," said Olor, somewhat suspiciously. "I thought he was about to destroy the last beech tree?"

"That's what I heard him saying," said Jack. "So he must still be in there. Let's be quick!"

"Without the GodMother, we don't have the strength to fight his army by ourselves," said Harold.

"Speak for yourself!" said Aiken, pulling a stick out of his belt as a weapon. Olor rolled her eyes at him.

"No, we need to be smarter than that," said Rowan. "We need to delay him until she arrives."

Aiken looked a little annoyed that he wasn't going to be able to take on the might of the foxes by himself.

"There is *one* thing that would stop him from destroying the tree," said Jack. "That is, if there were *no reason* to."

"No," said Harold, understanding before everyone else. "I don't like it."

"What does he mean?" whispered Willow to Rowan.

"He means me," said Rowan firmly. "He means, if Vulpes has got me, he doesn't need to do anything to the tree."

"But you can't—" began Olor.

"No, Jack's right," said Rowan. "I'm sure I could distract him for long enough."

"But we'll come with you!" said Aiken.

"No need to take that risk," said Rowan, shuddering to think what might happen to her sister if Vulpes got hold of her. "I can handle him. I've done it before."

"And while you do," said Jack, "I could sneak in and rescue your mother. I know where he's keeping her."

"Thank you, Jack," said Rowan, but it was clear that none of her friends agreed with the plan.

They were getting nearer to Vulpes's lair now. As they made their way through a copse on the side of a hill, they saw two great gnarled trees standing proudly a hundred meters away, silhouetted against the dark pre-dawn sky. A rustle nearby caused them to stop and hide behind a nearby tree. The dog sniffed the air, clearly detecting something. A fox suddenly broke cover, skulking away. They peered out from their hiding place to see the animal racing toward one of the great trees and disappearing into a hole beneath it.

"There," said Jack.

Everyone turned to look at Rowan.

"Are you sure?" asked Harold.

"Let's do this," said Rowan.

Rowan's mother had almost worked her bonds loose. A small strand of ivy was all that stood between her and freedom. She tugged with all her might to pull the last stem in two.

"You want to get back to your girls," said a familiar, disturbing voice from behind her.

Sylvia turned to see Vulpes brandishing a whole new vine of ivy, which he began wrapping around her arms to replace the one she had shaken off.

"I understand, of course I do," Vulpes continued. "But don't worry, I will *take care* of them both."

Rowan's mother felt sick, and shuddered involuntarily. Vulpes stretched out his wings and rose into the air.

"I can hear them from here, crashing about in the bushes. It's really not going to be much of a fight at all. I was hoping for a little more . . . entertainment."

"Rowan's too clever for you," snapped Sylvia.

"Not that smart at all, by the looks of it," replied Vulpes, pointing down into a clearing in front of their tree. Rowan's mother pushed forward to see what was happening. "No one should trust Jack Pike."

Her daughter was flying out into the clearing alone, lit only by a shaft of moonlight.

As Rowan glided out into the open, she started to have second thoughts. Maybe this wasn't such a good idea after all? She tried to push her worries to the back of her mind.

"I'm here, Vulpes," Rowan cried out into the darkness. "Just like you wanted. And I can help you."

"Rowan!" her mother cried out. "It's a trap!" Vulpes pushed her back into the tree out of sight, eyeing Rowan curiously from his treetop vantage point.

"Mom!" shouted Rowan, moving to meet the sound, before instinctively stopping herself.

"It's very kind of you to take me up on my invitation," said Vulpes. "So, how are you going to help me?"

Rowan could see Jack sneaking around the back of the tree, out of Vulpes's sight. She played for time.

"Because I have the secret. To turning back into a human. I can tell you how I did it."

"Come down to the hollow beneath this tree and

tell me all about it," he said. "I'll meet you there."

"No," replied Rowan firmly. "First I need to know that you won't destroy the weeping beech in Greenwich Park."

Vulpes raised an eyebrow.

"Well," he began, "haven't you become—how shall I put it—*strong-willed*?"

Rowan stood her ground.

"Why would I kill that tree anyway?" said Vulpes. "I was trying to stop you from becoming a fairy. And it looks like I've already failed on that score."

Rowan's doubts spread through her mind like a virus. Had Jack been telling them the truth?

"Where are your friends, Rowan?" Vulpes continued.

"I sent them home. This is just between you and me."

Vulpes stifled a laugh. "Priceless. I don't believe you for a second."

Rowan tried to stop her legs from shaking. She could see hundreds of orange eyes twinkling out from beneath the trees, restlessly bobbing up and down in constant movement.

"But it doesn't matter in the slightest," he continued. "Your zebra is stuck outside the park, your tiger is lame, and oh . . . I made a deal with your friend Jack while he was waiting for you."

Rowan felt her stomach drop.

"What kind of deal?"

"I told him he could have your mother back in exchange for you," said Vulpes. "Foxes!"

Vulpes raised his arms in the air, and the eyes became a huge army of foxes and fairy riders stalking out from their hiding places. Looking around, Rowan realized with dread that she was completely surrounded.

"Rowan!" she heard her mother scream from somewhere in the blackness.

Rowan turned to the sound, and in the distance she could see Jack hauling her struggling mother over the back of the hunting dog and disappearing into the night. Jack had betrayed them.

"NO! MOM!" she yelled back, beating her wings as hard as she could to give chase. But as she did so, a figure swooped in front of her to bar her way. Vulpes.

Chapter Twelve

THE EYE OF
THE STORM

"Don't think you're going to follow them," Vulpes said
smugly. "You're staying right here with me."

Rowan was furious.

"Get. Out. Of. My. Way," she snarled at him
through gritted teeth, desperate to get after Jack and
her mother. "Help! Harold!"

Vulpes held her back, which only made her angrier,
and she flailed her fists at him.

"Don't worry, little one," oozed Vulpes. "Jack will
look after her. Just like he always did. He's so very fond
of her. Just as well too, because I was starting to find
her quite dull."

"Aaaagh!" Rowan screamed in frustration, beating at his chest. "Aiken! Olor!"

"I really can't understand what you and he see in her, if I'm honest. But she was very useful in getting you here. And for that I am grateful."

Rowan's mother's screams were getting fainter and fainter. Rowan knew in her heart that Jack and her mother were long gone and there would be no finding them now. She stared off helplessly into the night. Where were her friends when she needed them? She soon found out.

A platoon of Fox Fairies marched her sister and her friends out into the clearing, their hands and wings bound behind their backs with ivy. Tigris was being set upon by a huge pack of slavering foxes, all taking bites at her tail and legs as she swung at them with her one good front paw.

"So, to business," announced Vulpes. "How *did* you transform back into a human?"

"Rowan!" shouted Willow. "Where's Mom?"

Rowan's heart broke for Willow, who hadn't seen her mother in seven years and had now had the opportunity ripped out of her grasp. If only Rowan had listened to Harold. She felt sick, and angry at herself for what had happened.

"It was a nice idea," said Vulpes, still entirely unmoved. "Bringing the tiger. Shame you couldn't find one that was less . . . feeble."

Rowan's blood was beginning to boil now, and she could feel the tingling rising up from her toes again. She felt a strength surge through her body, and she broke free of Vulpes's hold, kicking him in the chest and sending him reeling backward as she did so. She revolved in the air, trying to hold back the anger that she knew would get in her way. She began to spin faster and faster, and felt the familiar extension of her muscles and joints. What wasn't the same, though, was the extent of the sensation. It was like nothing she'd felt before. She had formed a picture in her mind and was willing the transformation with every fiber of her being. When she finally hit the ground and saw the looks on her friends' faces, she knew she'd managed it. Even the foxes all stopped and turned in shock. She was a tiger, a majestic white tiger. She opened her fearsome jaws wide, bared her fangs, and roared with all her might at Tigris's orange assailants.

"Attack!" she heard Vulpes shout from behind her, and that seemed to break his army out of its stunned state. They left poor Tigris stricken on the ground and turned on Rowan instead. What happened next took place almost in slow motion. Rowan fought on pure instinct, repelling the wave upon orange wave of foxes that crashed upon her. She thrashed some to the side with a paw, caught others in her powerful teeth and tossed them up into the air, and kicked others with her back legs, sending them rolling down the hill. The fight was a blur of action and reaction. In the chaos, Harold and the fairies broke free, to be joined by Fingers and Lutra, who had been hiding in a tree. The monkey and the otter freed the fairies from their bonds and enabled them to join the fray.

"Foxes!" came the cry from Vulpes.

And with that, Rowan saw hundreds more of the cunning creatures pouring into the clearing from all sides. It was like all the foxes in London were converging on this very point. Rowan wished that her sister and her friends would escape, but they didn't. They wouldn't leave Tigris's side, trying in vain to protect the animal from the new attackers. Rowan couldn't help them. Even as a tiger, she was being overwhelmed by the sheer number of the foxes coming at her.

But through the chaos Rowan saw her sister knocked to the ground. Unable to get to her, Rowan watched in horror as one great grizzled fox bounded toward her sister with its jaws hanging wide open. Time seemed to stand still, and all noise fell away. This was the moment she had dreaded. Rowan held her breath, frozen to the spot, but at the very last second Harold appeared from nowhere to put his body between the fox and Willow.

Instead of the fox's jaws closing around Willow, they snapped hard shut around the delicate body of the robin.

Rowan was paralyzed with shock as the fox's mouth opened again to let the bird roll out and fall to the ground.

Harold hit the earth with a thud. He wasn't moving.

Rowan refused to believe what her eyes were telling her. She struggled to throw off the foxes to go to him, but there were too many. She saw Willow bending down and reaching out an arm to touch him. Still he didn't move. She could see Willow turning to look at her with shock in her eyes, and in that moment Rowan knew there was no hope. She could feel a sickness rolling around in her stomach. A feeling of helpless desperation. She willed time to reverse. Anything to bring Harold back. Anything to stop this horrible feeling that she could have done something to stop it if only she'd had the chance. But she didn't have power over time. There was nothing she could do. What she had just witnessed had happened for real. And there was no changing it.

And with that, the anger returned.

It started with a rustling in the trees. Leaves starting to flutter. But it quickly grew stronger. A breeze that began by only brushing the faces of the fairies and the foxes became a gust of wind that rippled around the clearing, pushing branches this way and that. Rowan was unaware of it at first; she was still consumed with the fight at hand, though the sense of herself was different now. Her mind was no longer clear. On the contrary, it was entirely full. Full of frustration, and pain, and revenge. None of that made her a better fighter, but it certainly made her a stronger one. There were no holds barred now.

The gust became a gale as the wind picked up even further, blowing the trees bodily into one another and sending the other fairies reeling into the air. Willow, Aiken, and Olor grabbed on to a tree trunk and yelled at Rowan to stop, but she couldn't hear them. Rowan was still fighting in a rage—biting, pawing, and clawing anything that moved. There was a whirlwind around her now, with leaves and twigs whipped up from the ground being hurled into the sky with such force that Vulpes and the other fairies had to shield their eyes to protect themselves. A combination of Rowan's furious aggression and the violence of the wind had forced all the fairies and foxes back, to the point that now Rowan was alone in the middle of the clearing with Harold lying motionless on the ground, and Tigris incapacitated alongside. Rowan raised herself to full tiger height and let out a deafening roar of pent-up anger and pain. It was long and loud and seemed to go on forever, until finally she was spent. Like a raging fire that had burned itself out, she collapsed to the ground. Nothing left. The storm that had raged around her died too. And silence descended, along with a few solitary leaves that fluttered slowly to the ground.

Rowan found herself lying next to Harold. She was a fairy once more. The fight gone out of her, she wearily reached out to touch him, but felt no signs of life. A tear rolled out of her eye and landed on the dusty ground beneath her. As the moon shone down upon both of them, she started to sob.

A shape appeared above her, blocking out the silvery light. It was Vulpes, flanked by two great foxes that towered over her.

"It's finished," he said.

* Chapter Thirteen *
THE OBSERVATORY

From their hiding place behind a tree trunk, Willow, Aiken, and Olor could see a shattered Rowan being lifted to her feet by two of Vulpes's fairies and thrown over the back of a fox. They shrank back out of sight as Vulpes took one last look out over the clearing before disappearing off in the direction of the Royal Observatory, a pack of foxes following behind.

With the coast now clear, they emerged cautiously. Olor felt as weary as she had ever felt. Her body had already been weakened by the loss of the leaves on the weeping beech in the Park of St. James, so now the battle had really taken its toll. The fairies' wings made a mournful sound as they flew across to Harold and Tigris. The tiger was clearly hurt but was gradually able to stand.

"We need to get her to some humans. She needs the kind of help we can't give," said Olor.

Willow nodded. But first they had to take care of Harold. Holding him between them, they raised him and placed him gently onto Tigris's back. They sat with him nestled between the tiger's shoulder blades as she walked awkwardly forward on her injured paw. They passed through the trees, the fairies searching for the right place to lay him to rest, with Lutra and Fingers dragging behind them.

"There, look!" said Aiken, pointing toward a familiar-looking tree.

It was a weeping beech. Still intact. Olor smiled a sad smile.

Beneath the beech was the ancient, hollowed-out trunk of an oak tree lying on its side. They lifted Harold down from Tigris's back and gently placed him inside it, Lutra and Fingers scraping up a bed of leaves between them to cushion his body.

"Good-bye, beak face," said Aiken quietly, placing a large leaf over his friend's body.

A small tear ran down Olor's cheek.

"Good-bye, Harold," said Willow, repeating the gesture.

She took Aiken and Olor by the hands and squeezed. They squeezed her hands back. Still holding hands, they took one last look, one last deep breath, and then turned back to the tiger.

"Come on, Tigris," said Olor. "We need to get you home."

They made their way slowly down the hill through the park until they reached the gate Tigris had jumped over to get in. Spot had clearly long since departed.

"Now what?" asked Aiken.

"We wait with Tigris until she's safe," said Olor. "Then we find the GodMother."

"What about Rowan?" said Willow, stroking the tiger's great head.

"What can we do? The three of us?" replied Olor. "Against an army?"

"But what will he do to her?" asked Willow.

Olor looked at the ground. In all honesty she had no idea. But she doubted it would be good. Just then they heard the crackle of a walkie-talkie on the other side of the railings. A security guard was doing his rounds.

"Quick! Hide!" cried Olor, as loudly as she dared, before wincing in pain as she took off into the air, Lutra and Fingers scrambling for cover.

The fairies flew up into the nearest tree and looked on as the guard rounded a corner to see a tiger on the other side of the railing, lit from above by the streetlight. He slowly brought the walkie-talkie to his mouth.

"Dave," he said slowly. "Call the police. And the zoo."

The wind whistled through Rowan's hair as she looked out across the skyline of London. She felt the ivy bonds that Vulpes had tied her wings with digging into her flesh.

"Your mother liked this view," said Vulpes, pacing along the edge of the domed roof of the observatory. "Though, I much prefer having you here."

Rowan felt shattered. It was as if all the energy had been drained out of her body. She tried to muster up some kind of power to do something, anything, but all she wanted to do was rest.

"Come on, Rowan," said Vulpes. "Let's see one of your tricks! I want to know how it's done!"

But Rowan knew deep down that something had changed since the battle in the clearing. Whatever was inside her that enabled her to transform, to control nature, had burned itself out in that storm she'd created. In losing her mother again, and in losing Harold, she'd somehow lost the connection with her ability. All she felt now was tired.

"Finally we have no distractions," continued Vulpes. "No friends, no mothers, no need to fight. Just tell me the secret, and you can go too."

"There's no secret," replied Rowan. "There's nothing to tell you."

"Of course there is," said Vulpes. "How did you turn back into a human? You're the only fairy who's ever done it!"

"I would tell you if I knew," said Rowan. "Anything to get rid of you and your stupid battles, and your stupid anger."

Vulpes snickered to himself, and cocked an eyebrow at Rowan.

"Not something we could ever accuse you of? I'm

not sure it would have been quite so easy to catch you without *your* anger."

That touched a nerve for Rowan.

"Don't worry," he continued. "Anger is good! It makes things *happen*. Is that how you did it? Is that how you became human again?"

"No!" Rowan yelled. "Anger only makes bad things happen. I did everything I could to turn back into a human, and in the end, I don't know what I did. One minute I was a fairy, and the next I wasn't."

"Okay, my turn to get angry," said Vulpes. "Let's see what happens. Good or bad things?"

Vulpes grabbed Rowan and pushed her up against the railings on the edge of the roof, leaning her out over the three-story drop to the ground.

"I'm not going to ask you again. What. Did. You. DO!"

Rowan wasn't frightened of him. Instead she started to get riled up.

"Are you going to throw me off, then?" she said, spitting out the words. "Like you did with Aiken in the shopping center? Then you'll never know, will you?"

Rowan could see the blood rushing to Vulpes's head and felt his grip tightening around her, as he screamed right into her face, "You're useless! What good are you to anybody? Where are your friends and your family now, eh? They've all given up on you too! Tell me how to change back, or it ends here!"

"I'll tell you what I did, then!" Rowan yelled back at him, ripping off her treasured necklace and throwing it into his face. "The last thing I said before I changed back? I said 'I forgive you.' Why don't you try that? Why don't you try *forgiving* someone and see what that does!"

Vulpes let the wooden pendant bounce off him and slide down the domed roof below. He released his grip on Rowan. He went very quiet. Rowan straightened up.

"That would be tricky for you, wouldn't it?" asked Rowan, beginning to enjoy herself a little now. "You're desperate to be human to get your revenge on your uncle, but if forgiveness really is the key . . . well, you're a bit stuck, aren't you?"

Vulpes was positively seething now. It looked like his brain was going to boil over.

"Do you know what, Rowan? It doesn't matter. If that's how you did it, I can find another way."

Rowan wasn't sure where Vulpes was going with this.

"You know, I've noticed the fairies getting weaker," he continued. "It's the leaves, isn't it? When I stripped all the leaves from the weeping beeches, I was really just doing it to stop you from getting your silly powers back. But it's had some rather delicious side effects, hasn't it?"

Rowan was incredulous.

"You mean you've enjoyed seeing fairies in pain?"

"Rowan, don't you see? The fairies' wings are disintegrating. We're becoming more . . . human."

"But—but you don't know what it's really doing to us! What if it's *killing* the fairies instead?" said Rowan.

Vulpes tilted his head to one side to think. A demonic smile crept across his face as he raised himself to his full height.

"You're right. It's a gamble, isn't it?"

"But that's insane! I won't let you!"

Vulpes leaned in close and whispered malevolently into Rowan's ear, "I'm afraid there's nothing you can do." And with that he shoved Rowan bodily through the railings, sending her tumbling down the dome.

Everything went black.

* Chapter Fourteen *
ALL IS LOST

Rowan heard noises first. Airplanes flying way overhead, trees creaking in the breeze. Then she felt the
wind on her face as it murmured around her. And then
came the horrible sick feeling in the pit of her stomach when she remembered that Harold was gone. It
hadn't been a dream. It was real.

She slowly opened her eyes, and immediately flinched
when she realized where she was. Rowan was balanced
precariously on the edge of a narrow balcony at the bottom of the great domed roof of the Royal Observatory.
She lifted her head, careful not to overbalance herself and
fall through the white wooden railings to the ground ten
meters below. As she raised her head, she spotted her
necklace draped forlornly across the balustrade above
her. She instinctively beat her wings to fly up to grab it,

but grimaced with pain as she realized her wings were still bound by the ivy strands Vulpes's henchmen had tied them with. The fall had loosened the bonds, however, and she was soon able to wriggle them off. Soaring into the air, she gratefully gathered the necklace from its perch. She clattered back to the balcony, panting from the effort. She was still weak, and the fall had hurt her more than she'd realized. Fixing the pendant around her neck again, she looked out through the railings into the night. Vulpes was nowhere to be seen. Where were her friends? She decided to return to the scene of the battle and start there.

Rowan took a deep breath and launched herself through the gap into the void. Her wings spread wide and caught a gust of wind that immediately knocked her off balance, spinning her sideways and crashing her into a bush below. She dusted herself off and half-flew, half-hopped along the grass back toward the clearing.

A fox howled somewhere in the distance, but there was none to be seen when she made it back to Vulpes's tree. It was like the world had emptied out and she was the only one left in it. Where were Willow, and Aiken, and Olor and the beasts? Where in the Realms had Jack taken her mom? And what had become of Harold's body?

She had never felt more alone than in that moment, never less sure of what to do next. A little way down the hill, she saw a weeping beech standing above a fallen tree trunk. *I'm too late,* she thought. The tree was completely bare and creaked pitifully in the wind. *I've failed.* As she drew nearer, rain started to fall. At first she raised her face to meet the droplets, trying to let the water wash away her pain. She breathed in that familiar smell that her mother loved so much. But then the rain began to fall harder, beating the ground around her. She quickly took shelter within the hollowed-out trunk lying at the foot of the beech.

And then Rowan realized that she was not alone. Her breath caught in her throat and she let out a cry of shock. It was Harold, laid out where Willow, Aiken, and Olor had left him beneath the leaves. The tears came immediately. She couldn't stop them. She held his body tight and wept for a second time. Only now his feathers were cold. A hard rain drummed off the log above them.

"We're lost," said Jack.

They had been pounding the streets for what seemed like hours, and Jack clearly had no idea where they were.

It had begun to rain. Rowan's mother lifted her face to the sky to meet it, but instead of making her happy as it always used to, it only made her fearful. Because it reminded her of Rowan and Willow, somewhere out there in the night. And she didn't know whether or not they were safe. There was nothing that made her feel worse than that.

The hunting dog was jittery. It paced back and forth beneath them as Jack tried to make up his mind which way they should go. Sylvia looked this way and that—something looked familiar to her about where they were, but she wasn't about to start helping Jack find his way, after what he'd done. She strained against the ivy tying her hands and wings behind her back, trying to twist and turn to release herself from the knots.

"Please just let me go, Jack," said Rowan's mom as calmly as she could.

"After the trouble I've gone to? To make you safe? I'm fixing things."

"How are you doing that?"

"I rescued you from Vulpes," he replied. "Ever since your troublemaker daughter fell in, everything's gone to the foxes. She was going to get you killed, and I saved you."

"But she's my daughter, Jack! My flesh and blood! I want to be with her! And Willow, and my husband."

Jack snorted with laughter. "Fat lot of good *they've* all been to you."

Sylvia screamed with frustration, but the sound was quickly drowned out by a car racing toward them down the street. She and Jack both turned at the noise, momentarily blinded by the car's approaching headlights. She seized her chance while he was distracted.

"I've had enough of being told what to do," she said, and slipped off the dog's back. She ran awkwardly into a pitch-black side street, which seemed to be lined with enormous rubbish bins. It stank, but that was the least of her worries. She ducked behind the farthest one and tried to wriggle free of her bonds.

"Sylvia, where *are* you?" Jack was yelling from the other end of the side street. "It's time to go home!" He was getting closer.

She could feel her heart beating so hard that it was almost pounding out of her chest. Then she heard a rustle behind her. She spun around in an instant. Had Jack found her? No! A FOX! She recoiled in shock, frantically pulling at the ivy holding her wrists. The fox snapped its jaws at her, missing her by millimeters. All at once the ties fell to the ground, and she shot into the air like a firework. She soared over the dark buildings, leaving Jack searching for her below. Thank the GodMother he didn't look up at just that moment. . . .

She banked to the left, back down the main street they'd been on, toward a very familiar-looking apartment building. It was the first time she'd seen it in seven years. It was her old apartment. Muddleheaded Jack really had brought her home. Only, not the one he'd intended to.

She flew up high, searching for the right window. It was still so early in the morning, the curtains were drawn in virtually all of them. Finally she came across a disheveled-looking man wearing a dressing gown over the clothes he must have been wearing the whole day before. It looked like he hadn't been to sleep all night. He was staring into the distance as if he were in a trance. It couldn't be her husband? She rapped on the window until his reverie was broken.

Rowan's dad rubbed his eyes to make sure that he hadn't fallen asleep after all.

"Sylvia?" he whispered in disbelief.

Rowan's mom, reading his lips through the glass, nodded.

He carefully opened the window, and she hovered into the room. He gently cupped his hand around her in the closest thing to a fairy embrace. She looked up at him, hardly believing what was happening herself.

"Welcome home," he said.

Never before had those two simple words meant so much to Sylvia, and a flood of tears rushed down her cheeks. But she knew they couldn't stay here together, not just yet at least.

"Ted," she said, drying her eyes. "The children."

"Do you know where they are?" he asked, suddenly alert.

Sylvia nodded. "Can we go to them? Now? I'll explain everything on the way."

Ted looked at his long-lost wife, now a fairy resting in his palm, then glanced down at his dressing gown.

"This is the strangest dream I've ever had," he said. "But I really don't want to wake up."

The rain had slowed to a patter on the tree trunk, but Rowan's tears were still falling heavily onto the cold feathers of her friend.

"It's all my fault, Harold," she said, as if he could still hear her.

She stroked his head, trying to believe that he was just sleeping.

"I let Willow get into danger, I let Jack take Mom, I couldn't stop Tigris from getting hurt, and worst of all, I wasn't there for you, and . . . *this* is what happened. I'm so sorry, Harold. It was up to me, and I failed. Completely."

She looked up at the dark, shifting clouds above their heads, and felt the wind rising around them. It threw the rain droplets into her face like little darts, stinging her cheeks. She shielded her face as the gusts grew stronger, lifting leaves and twigs from the ground and hurling them around the trunk like clothes in a tumble dryer. Rowan wasn't the one causing the gale this time, and she pressed herself against the inside of the trunk to try to shelter from it. She closed her eyes as if she could shut out the pain, but her attempt only seemed to lock the pain inside. She beat her fists against the trunk, slowly at first, then harder and faster until she howled in anguish.

"AGHHHHHH!" she yelled into the wind. And as quickly as the wind had risen, it fell still just as swiftly. She slipped down the curved wall of wood and slumped into a heap at the bottom, curled up like a baby in a crib. There were no tears left now. She just felt numb and alone. A tiny fairy lost in the darkness, in a part of the city she didn't know.

She heard a rustle in the leaves behind her. Her head dropped. She prayed it wasn't a fox. She slowly turned to see where the noise was coming from. All at once she knew something was wrong. Harold's body had gone. But there was something else there, with her, in the tree trunk. Something alive.

Chapter Fifteen

HAROLD IS ME

There was another movement at the far end of the trunk, but it was pitch-black back there, and however much she strained her eyes, Rowan couldn't make anything out. She tried to stop herself from trembling.

"Who's there?" she said, as confidently as she could muster.

No voice came back. Only the sound of something shifting in the darkness.

"What have you done with Harold?"

And then whatever it was moved toward her. A figure emerged from the shadows. A fairy of the birds, the same height as Rowan, in a feathered cloak, brown all over save for his chest, which burned a deep red.

"Harold is here," it said. In Harold's voice. "Harold is me."

Rowan instinctively backed away from the figure, not ready to accept that what he said could possibly be the truth. And if he wasn't Harold, who or what was he?

The fairy calling himself Harold clearly understood what Rowan was feeling, and stopped in his tracks.

"Don't be afraid of me, Rowan," said the fairy.

Rowan flinched.

"You can't be Harold. Harold died. I saw it happen with my own eyes."

"A part of me died, that's true. But this is who I always was."

Rowan wasn't quite ready to believe what he was saying, but she'd stopped trying to get away from him. He had a kind face, but she'd trusted Jack and that hadn't turned out well. . . .

"It is"—he spread his arms wide—"what it is."

Rowan froze.

"Let me tell you my story, Rowan," he continued. "Please, sit down."

Rowan considered a moment. She wanted so much for this to be Harold; that he might still be alive. She slowly lowered herself to the ground to listen to what he had to say.

"You asked me once what I was. Was I a fairy or a bird? And I said I was a bird granted the gift of speech."

Rowan felt a shiver go through her. Surely only Harold could know that he'd said that to her?

"But it wasn't the whole truth," he continued. "Actually, I was stuck. Trapped between forms. Neither fairy nor bird."

"But, how?" asked Rowan.

Harold paused. Rowan could tell that whatever he was about to say wasn't going to be easy for him.

"It started when I fell into the Realms," he said. "I was young, and I'd fallen in love. I loved a girl with all my heart, but her parents wouldn't let us be together. I came into St. James's Park, and I wept beneath the beech, just like you did in Hyde Park. And I became a fairy. And, just like you, I was desperate to return to the human world. I wasn't ready to leave the girl I loved, wasn't ready to give up. My soul was restless, and so I had the power of transformation. The GodMother warned me against it, but I wouldn't listen. I turned into a robin and flew out of the park to find her again."

Harold's head dropped. It was getting harder for him to speak. Rowan edged closer.

"Go on," she urged.

"I landed on her windowsill. I was trying to find a way to get in, but then I saw her. With someone else. Someone else she was clearly in love with. It wasn't her parents who didn't want us to be together; it was her. But she never had the heart to tell me."

Rowan felt a lump come up in her throat. She could feel how much it had hurt him. How much it still did.

"So I flew back to the GodMother and told her I no longer had any desire to return to the human world. And with that desire went my restlessness. And with that restlessness went my power to transform. Only my ability to speak remained. The GodMother was wise, as she always is. She sent me to be with the Fairies of the Trees, who didn't know what had happened to me. She thought I could start a new life there and perhaps in time I would become a fairy again. But I never did. Until now."

"But why now, Harold?" Rowan said his name without even thinking about it. Her heart had told her the truth before her head had realized. Harold smiled at the sound of his name from her lips.

"Emotions are powerful things in the Realms,

Rowan. They can trap you, and they can set you free. I can't say for sure, but I think it was you. Your tears that released me. Your . . . love."

Rowan rose and hugged him.

"Thank you, Rowan," he whispered into her ear.

She squeezed him tighter. She had no words that could possibly describe the joy she felt in knowing he was alive.

"And know this," he said softly. "None of what happened is your fault. Not to me, not to you or Willow, not to your mother. You don't bear the weight by yourself. No one can. You don't have to be angry anymore."

She could feel her despair slowly trickling away, and hope beginning to fill her up again.

"Rowan!" came a shout in the distance.

"ROWAN!" Another, closer this time.

It couldn't be, could it? It sounded just like . . .

"DAD!"

Rowan and Harold soared out from inside the tree trunk. The rain had stopped, and the clouds were parting to reveal a brightness in the east. Dawn was on its way. Rowan and Harold flew straight up so that they could quickly see where the voice was coming from. A taxi's headlights swept across the park in a great curve as it turned to head back out down the road. A figure was walking toward Rowan and Harold.

"Come on!" said Rowan to Harold, darting ahead, all weakness and injury forgotten in the happiness of seeing her dad walking toward them.

Rowan was flying so fast, she practically crashed into him.

"Dad!" she cried.

"Oh, Rowan," said Dad, cradling her gently to his chest as a face appeared from out of his pocket.

"Mom! But how?"

"I suppose we've all got some surprises up our sleeves," said Sylvia, hugging Rowan.

Rowan's heart practically burst out of her chest with pride and joy. Throughout everything that had happened to her over the seven years since her mother had disappeared, this was the one thing that she'd almost not dared to dream might happen—that she might be together with her parents again. But here they were.

Although, of course there was someone still missing.

"Where's Willow, Rowan?" asked Sylvia.

"I don't know," admitted Rowan, her head dropping. "I—I lost her."

"She won't be far," said Dad, trying to reassure her. "She can look after herself as well as you can, I'm sure."

Rowan hoped he was right. But a howl in the distance sent a shot of fear through her.

"It must be Vulpes," said Rowan. "Follow me."

She sprang off in the direction of the sound, her mom and dad giving chase. More howls screamed out into the dawn light, and foxes began to appear all around them. Not running at them but running past them instead, in a snarling mass of rusty fur. Urged on by fox fairy riders, they were all converging—on the observatory.

Chapter Sixteen

TURNING THE TABLES

High up on the dome of the observatory, Vulpes stood triumphantly, the glint of morning sun reflecting madly in his eyes. His arms were stretched out wide, as if he were welcoming home an old friend.

"I'm ready to grow!" he shouted to the sky above. "Let loose these wings and let me be human again!"

Vulpes started tugging at his wings as if trying to pull them off. Then he saw Rowan staring up at him.

"There you are," he said. "I wanted you to be the first to see me become a man again."

The assembled crowd of foxes and their riders howled in appreciation.

"It won't work!" shouted Rowan.

"Just. Need. More. Time," said Vulpes, still trying to pull furred feathers from his wings.

"It won't work because there's a tree you've missed!" came a shout from somewhere behind them all.

Everyone turned to see who'd said it.

On the back of his hunting dog was Jack.

"Because there's another tree," said Jack. "In the Realm of the Tree Fairies. We're all weaker now that you've destroyed those trees, but it's the last one in all the Realms that will break the curse and restore fairies to their human form."

"IS THIS TRUE?" Vulpes roared at Rowan.

Rowan's mind whirred. One thing was sure, though, being a fairy wasn't a curse. Harold flew in front of Rowan as if to protect her from Vulpes's wrath.

"You won't find it," said Harold.

"Whoever *you* are," replied Vulpes, "you're bluffing."

"I'll show you where it is!" cried Jack.

"No!" shouted Sylvia. "Haven't you done enough damage?"

Everyone turned back to Jack in disgust. Apart from Vulpes, of course.

"I always liked you, Jack," oozed Vulpes. "You know which side your bread is buttered on."

"Follow me!" yelled Jack, turning the dog around and whipping off down the hill.

Vulpes and the foxes gave chase en masse. Rowan and her family looked on despondently. She couldn't believe that Jack could betray them a second time. And in such a terrible way.

"Wait a second," said Harold. "What's he doing now?"

Rowan looked up to see Jack leading the foxes into a giant hollow halfway down the hill, and then suddenly stopping at the bottom of it. She flew after them to see what was happening.

"Why have you stopped?" Vulpes shouted at Jack as the foxes all swarmed around him.

"Now!" screamed Jack, and a flock of great white swans rose up from the rim of the hollow above the foxes. Riding on the necks of the angry birds were Olor and the GodMother. Rappelling down from the trees above was Aiken, leading a troop of Tree Fairies brandishing sticks. And then, thundering around behind the foxes to cut off their retreat was a herd of deer ridden by russet-furred Deer Fairies and led by Willow riding Spot the zebra. Jack had led the foxes into a trap!

"FOXES!" yelled Vulpes in an attempt to rally his orange army, huddling together like frightened sheep in a pen. "Attack!"

But before they could muster any kind of response, a deafening roar heralded a truly astonishing sight. Bounding into the hollow was a giant black gorilla, ridden by Simeon himself. In a single movement it barreled into the mass of foxes, skittering them left and right. The ones that didn't immediately scatter were hurled headlong into the undergrowth. Like a baby throwing toys out of a crib, the gorilla whirled the yelping beasts over its head, sending them flying into bushes and bouncing off tree trunks. Rowan looked on in amazement as Vulpes's army was picked off before her eyes. The fairies that had been riding the foxes took flight and were chased off by the swans, their beaks snapping at their heels until the fairies disappeared off into the retreating night. The stray foxes that remained were driven down the hill by Spot the zebra and his army of deer. It was a total rout. The gorilla finally stopped, stood, and beat its chest in victory.

"We've won!" shouted Aiken.

"I couldn't let you have all the entertainment to yourselves," said Simeon.

Rowan looked around her, not quite believing it could have been possible.

"Where's Vulpes?" Rowan asked, suddenly realizing he'd vanished.

"Gone forever?" replied Aiken hopefully.

"Not yet," said the GodMother, sliding down the neck of her swan onto the ground next to Rowan. "He's still close by. You must find him, Rowan."

Rowan nodded. This was between her and Vulpes now. And she knew where he was going to be.

"Stay here," she told her family. "I'll be right back."

"Hang on," said Aiken, pointing at Harold. "Who's this?"

"No time," she replied. "I'll let him explain!"

Leaving a rather sheepish Harold in her wake, Rowan flew swiftly back toward the observatory, and sure enough, there was Vulpes, sitting on his favorite perch, on top of the dome looking out over London. He leapt up immediately when he saw Rowan, and glided awkwardly down to the ground to meet her.

He looked tired, and jerked left and right awkwardly, as if his wings weren't working properly.

"It's still happening," he said. "Maybe we haven't destroyed all the weeping beeches in the Realms, but the weakness is coming. My wings are failing. I'm going to do what you did. I'm going to be human again too."

Rowan just stared at him. Was he going completely mad? She was almost beginning to feel sorry for the deluded dark fairy.

"It's not happening, Vulpes. It's not the way," said Rowan.

"I'll find the last tree. I'll finish the job if I have to do it myself!"

"It's over, Vulpes. You've lost."

"No!" he shouted, refusing to accept the truth.

Was that a tear she could see in his eye? She stepped closer to him.

"I'm sorry if you can't be human again, Vulpes. I know how much it means to you."

He was still darting left and right, becoming more and more erratic as the desperation set in. He flew right up to her face, so close that she could see the madness in his eyes.

"You want to be rid of me, don't you? What are you going to do about it, then?" He seemed to read her mind.

Rowan somehow knew in that precise moment that she could be rid of him. If she wanted to. She could transform into some great creature and swat him like a fly. After all the pain he'd caused the Realms, she could be the one to free them from him once and for all. The burden would lift from her shoulders. She felt the anger in her rise like flames.

Vulpes was almost smiling now. He seemed to be willing her to do it. He wanted fire to meet fire. And then something opened in her mind that fought the flames. He seemed to sense it.

"You can't do it, can you? You don't have the strength to do it."

Rowan knew instantly what she must do instead. It felt absolutely, instinctively right. As the GodMother had told her, "The best cure for fire is water."

"I forgive you, Vulpes."

"Agh!" He let out a scream of exasperation. "No one understands. What it's like. To be me."

And with that, he spun in the air and hit the ground

as a fox, chest heaving up and down. He snarled at her, curling back his lips to reveal his sharp, yellowed teeth. It should have been Rowan's turn to be fearful now, but instead of recoiling, Rowan remained impassive and unafraid. Because she felt an almighty energy surging through her. She began to rise, growing taller, wider, heavier. Her wings receded into her body. Every muscle in her body ached, every bone stretched, until finally she towered above the fox. *As a human.* It felt so natural, she hardly skipped a beat.

"You're right," she said. "No one can truly know what it's like to be you. But I know what it's like to be in pain. And I know you'll never be free of it until you let go." She stepped closer and held out her hand. "Let go of everything."

She reached out to touch his head and gently stroke his fur, just as if he were a family dog. At first the fox shivered, cringing away from the human who had for the second time just achieved his most fervent dream. But then, just for a moment, she felt his head rise to her touch, letting himself be comforted. Then he quickly pulled back, snarling again. He rolled and spun, as if trying to transform back into a fairy. But nothing happened. He chased his tail in frustration, leapt, and yelped. Still nothing. He seemed stuck. Just as Harold had been stuck as a bird, he was trapped as a fox.

"Go," she said. "Go and don't come back."

Vulpes growled a low growl. And then he spoke as a fox, just as Harold had been able to speak as a bird.

"Maybe you do understand," he said, "better than I do."

He stood there for a moment, just looking at her, as if he didn't quite know what to do next. Then slowly, very slowly, he bowed his head, like a courtier acknowledging a queen, before turning tail and bounding away. She watched him streak down the hill, out of the park, into the morning light. Was that the last she would see of him? The last anyone would see of him?

* Chapter Seventeen *
THE SECRET

"You did something amazing," said Harold. "The right thing,"

"Becoming human again?" Rowan replied.

Harold smiled at her and shook his head. "Letting Vulpes go."

Rowan breathed deeply, glad for the reassurance from her friend. The sun was now fully visible in the sky, sending shafts of bright light bouncing around the park.

"Come on," said Harold. "The gates to the park are open now. People could be here any minute. And there's something else you need to do before they arrive."

They hurried back to the sorry-looking weeping beech, past the odd fox slinking away with its tail between its legs. Her dad was cradling Rowan's fairy mother and sister in his hands, but when they noticed her approaching, Dad held out his arms for Rowan to join the embrace.

"Look," Rowan's mother said gazing up at her daughter. "Look how you've grown."

Rowan's heart swelled to feel Willow reunited with their mother at last. She remembered how she had felt at that exact same moment. But she was filled with a new sensation now. The feeling of a whole family reunited, holding one another tightly in the best way that they could. Two humans and two fairies, yes, but one family all together again.

Jack was lingering nearby and finally approached.

"I'm sorry," said Jack.

Sylvia and Willow instinctively hid behind Rowan's dad.

"I was wrong," said Jack. "I needed to make amends. To do the right thing for once."

"Jack," said Rowan. "I forgive you. Thank you for helping us be together again."

Rowan's dad put his arm around her. Jack nodded his acknowledgment, before stumbling and having to sit down. He looked weary, ill even.

"Are you okay, Jack?"

Jack held up a hand. "Just need a little rest."

Rowan looked around and realized that the other fairies were the same. Simeon was lying with his back against a tree. Olor was being tended by a concerned Aiken. Even the GodMother seemed to have aged ten years in an evening.

"GodMother, what can we do?" asked Rowan.

"You need to go to your home," said the God-Mother. "Get away from this sickness while you can."

"How is that even possible? How could we leave you all like this? Leave the Realms in ruins?"

The joy of her family being reunited was evaporating rapidly. The enormity of what still needed to be done was growing by the second. The Realms were in tatters, and her family would never truly be together until Rowan's mother and sister were human again too.

"You have more power within you than I ever thought possible," said the GodMother. "So maybe you can achieve it. . . ."

"Achieve what?" asked Rowan urgently.

"The *impossible*," replied the GodMother, slumping onto the ground, exhausted.

"No!" Rowan was starting to panic, holding the GodMother's tiny face in her fingers, trying to rub life back into it. "This can't happen. Harold!"

Harold rushed over and held the GodMother's wrist to feel her pulse. "It's very weak, Rowan. You have to do something quickly."

"Yes, but what?" replied Rowan.

"The trees, Rowan," said Harold. "You have a power over nature. Surely there must be something you can do?"

A feather dropped from his own fairy wing and fluttered to the ground.

Rowan turned to face the great, bare tree above them. She closed her eyes and held her arms in the air as much in hope as in expectation. However much she willed it, nothing happened. "My powers were as a fairy, not as a human," she said. "There's nothing I can do."

Rowan was distraught. She felt Harold's tiny hand against her cheek. "You don't bear the weight on your own."

Willow appeared next to them. "I'll help you, Rowan."

Rowan smiled down at her sister.

"What can I do?" asked her mom.

"And me?" asked her dad.

"I don't think you—" But then Rowan stopped in her tracks, her brain buzzing. "Thank you. All of you. Maybe you *can* help. Hold my hands."

The family clasped one another's hands in the best way they could.

"What are you doing?" asked Harold.

"The beeches, they transform the unloved," said Rowan.

"Yes?" Harold looked confused still.

"So the energy within them must be the opposite," said Rowan "It must *be* love. If we want to cure the trees, perhaps we just have to fill them back up with that energy. It worked for you."

Harold smiled as the family held hands. Two humans and two fairies reaching as far as they could around the ancient tree. Rowan closed her eyes and felt a warmth surging through her. The love of her reunited family. She looked up at the tree. Was anything changing?

"Something is blocked," said Rowan. "I can feel it. That's why it isn't working. I'm sure of it."

"Complete the circle and reach all the way around the tree," said Harold. "Perhaps that will help?"

"But we could only do that by . . ." Rowan trailed off.

"Becoming human again," said Sylvia, finishing her daughter's sentence.

"How did you . . . ?" Willow began.

Rowan was already way ahead of her. The pieces had finally all fallen into place.

"I know what the riddle means," said Rowan, instinctively reaching for her necklace.

All eyes were on her.

"When the fairy of most power unlocks the Heart of Oak, they shall become human again."

"But it's not a riddle," replied Aiken, even more confused.

"We never thought it was, but perhaps it is," said Rowan. "The Heart of Oak is the heart of someone who feels unloved. That is the feeling that turns us into fairies in the first place. The power we have to set it free is love and . . . forgiveness."

Harold smiled and nodded. It all made sense. Rowan warmed to her idea.

"I forgave Vulpes, and I changed back," said

Rowan. Then she looked to her mother. "And it's what happened the first time too. I was just looking down, through the rushing water, to see you and my friends below. The last thing I said was . . . 'I forgive you, Mom.'"

A tear slipped quickly down her mother's cheek. She seemed almost in shock.

"What did you mean," her mom said, choking back the emotion, "by what you said?"

"I meant that I understood why you left. That you were sad. And that it was okay."

Sylvia squeezed Rowan's finger tightly as Willow jumped up.

"I'm a fairy because I ran away," said Willow. "I was upset and angry with you, Rowan. I'm sorry. I know you were only trying to look after me."

Rowan almost spluttered. "How can I undo that feeling for you when it's really my fault? Me thinking you were getting in the way, when you've done nothing but help and make me proud of you."

"I forgive you, Rowan," said Willow, simply and quietly.

Without any fanfare Willow began to grow. Her

wings shrank away to nothing, and within seconds she was back to human size. Willow held out her hands to examine them as if to make sure they were still hers. Then she jumped on top of Rowan in glee, giving her a joyous hug. It was like being attacked by a large cuddly dog. Rowan hugged her back, but the day was breaking and the job wasn't done.

"Hold on, Willow. We're not finished!" said Rowan, half-laughing.

They still couldn't reach all the way around the tree.

"Mom, you can change back too," said Rowan urgently. "Say you forgive me."

"I've nothing to forgive you for, Rowan. You've done nothing wrong." Rowan's mother was bereft. "You're just a beautiful, loving child who needed her mom to be there for her."

"Say you forgive *me*?" said Rowan's dad suddenly. "Wasn't it my fault you cried beneath the weeping beech that day? Wasn't it my fault you became a fairy in the first place?"

Rowan's mother shook her head. "Of course I would forgive you if there were anything for you to be sorry for. But there really isn't, my love. My sadness was like a storm cloud that blew in one day and soaked me to the skin. There was no rhyme nor reason. And no one to blame."

Clearly nothing was happening, and the sun was getting higher in the sky. The gates to the park were open now, and the public would soon flood in again.

"Thank you, Rowan," said Mom. "But I just don't think I can turn back. There's no one to forgive. Because this was all my fault, no one else's." She stroked Rowan's thumb as a tear made its way down her cheek. "I'm sorry, Rowan. I'm sorry I can't be who you want me to be."

"You *are* who I want you to be, Mom! You always were. The person you have to forgive is *yourself*. For even thinking that."

Rowan's mom wiped the tear from her cheek and stood up straighter, as if a weight were somehow lifting from her. Rowan took heart and continued, holding out the oak pendant to show her mom. There was the acorn and the oak tree, inextricably linked, one to the other.

"You bought this, Mom," said Rowan. "You understood. We're a part of each other. The Heart of Oak means more for us than just a riddle. It's a symbol of the bond we share. I forgive you, Mom. Say that you forgive yourself too. Please."

Sylvia shook her head. "I can't. . . ."

"*Please*, Mom."

Sylvia seemed to understand.

"Okay," she whispered. She seemed to gather herself for a moment, before taking a deep breath. "I forgive . . . myself."

Almost instantly Sylvia began to grow in front of Rowan's eyes. Her wings shrank back into her body, her limbs extended, and she was *laughing* as if it were the most ridiculous thing in the world. Rowan held her mother's gaze all the way, following her growth upward until finally her mother was taller than her. Sylvia was human again. Her mom reached over and drew her family into an enormous hug.

"Thank you, Rowan. Thank you for bringing me back."

An incredible feeling of well-being flooded through Rowan. She felt the warmth of happiness flow around her. They were ready.

"Hold hands. Reach around the tree," she said to her family.

Now all human size, their arms reached around with ease. They all closed their eyes. Rowan focused like she had never done before, on all that she had learned, on all that she had felt, on all that she wanted to happen. And she felt something, not fairy power this time but something else. Love.

"It's working!" she heard Aiken shout.

She opened her eyes and looked up. Up in the weeping beech, tiny buds were forming before their very eyes. It was like one of those nature programs where they speed everything up, except it was happening for real. Bright new green leaves unfurled and shook themselves loose. In an instant the tree was fully restored, shimmering spring green in the summer's dawn light, branches gently swaying in the breeze.

"GodMother!" said Olor as the old fairy wearily came to.

The GodMother looked up into the canopy. "You've brought us back," she said to Rowan. "The trees are returning across the Realms. I can feel it. Rejuvenation. Because of you."

Rowan saw all her friends beaming up at her.

"You could come back with me?" she said hopefully. "To the human world. Now that we know how?"

"Our home is here in the Realms," said Aiken. "Most of us don't have as much to go back for as you," he added, a touch sadly.

"It is what it—" Harold began.

"But there'll always be a home for you here, too," interrupted Olor.

Rowan looked over to see her family. Her fairy friends and her human family were now worlds apart. And she realized that this was the moment when she had to say good-bye. She crouched down to be closer to the fairies.

"It's time for me to go home," she said, not quite believing what she was saying. It was all happening so fast. Was she really ready to leave her friends behind? She couldn't begin to express what they had all done for her. "I—I . . ."

Harold seemed to know what she wanted to say.

"We'll miss you too, Rowan."

Rowan cupped Harold in her hands and smiled down at him. "I promise I'll come back, if ever you need me," she said.

"I'll be a fairy again too!" cried Willow from behind her sister.

They all grinned at one another, just as they heard the sound of a van roaring into the park in the distance. Rowan turned and could just about make out the logo of London Zoo on its side. It really was time to go now. Jack bid farewell to his hunting dog. Willow did the same to Spot. Aiken and Olor said good-bye to Fingers and Lutra. Simeon hid himself deep in the gorilla's fur, ready for the return trip to the zoo. Rowan felt a tiny jolt as Harold pushed away from her hand and lifted into the air. She watched him and her other fairy friends rise slowly and silently into the trees above, waving as they went. When at last they had all disappeared into the foliage, Rowan joined hands with her reunited family and started walking down the hill toward the Thames and a riverboat that would take them home. She paused to steal one last look out across London in the morning light. And took a great breath in.

Rowan breathed out staring at that same view, but from high up in the air this time. They were back at their apartment. All together for the first time in seven years. They all sat back in their old familiar chairs. Dad, Willow, Rowan, and now Mom in her chair that faced the window, looking out and away. But Rowan could tell that her mom felt something wasn't quite right. Sylvia lifted the chair and turned it around to face her family instead of the view.

"Much better," she said.

And she smiled.

Acknowledgments

I have been on almost as much of a journey as Rowan has over the course of the two books I've now written about her and her adventures, and there's a number of people I would like to thank for the support they've given me along the way.

Firstly, Alyson Heller, Emma Sector, and the team at Aladdin for being such supporters of Rowan and me; our talented illustrator Jori van der Linde, who has brought Tigris so wonderfully to life. Claire Wilson and Miriam Tobin at Rogers, Coleridge and White, because there's nothing more reassuring than knowing someone is looking out for you.

My parents, John and Lynda Clarke, and my family and friends who've gone out of their way to buy, recommend, and spread the word about the book—which has been such an unexpected and humbling pleasure. My wife, Rachel Clarke, who has not only been a constant support, but a fabulous first copy editor and social media adviser to boot.

And finally, I'd like to dedicate this book to the memory of my wife's beloved mother, Hilary Bishop.

She delighted in sending book one far and wide, and was so pleased to show her friends her name in the acknowledgments. She never got to read this one, but I hope she would have been just as proud.

About the Author

E. J. CLARKE decided to write *Oakwing*, his first novel, after the idea popped into his head and wouldn't leave. He lives in North London and is married with two young daughters who would like to be fairies. He hopes these books will give them that chance. When he's not writing about fairies, he works for a company that makes films and television programs.